BITE OF JUSTICE

BLOOD OATH
BOOK FOUR

R.L. CAULDER

WHITE RABBIT PUBLISHING

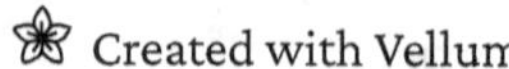 Created with Vellum

For Lauren Cox—Who rocks my fucking socks.

I couldn't think of a better person to dedicate this final book in the series to.

Thank you for single-handedly breathing life back into my muse with your excitement and support of this series. I honestly don't think I could have started this book without your determination to make me believe in myself. You told my imposter syndrome to STFUATTDLAGG.

Your love for me and these characters is something I'll always hold close to my heart. Forever grateful for you, my Princess. (Not Lincoln's).

Love, R.L.

CHAPTER ONE
ALINA

The wind howled, an eerie whistle, and a rumble like distant drums filled the air. Rain pelted down like a million tiny pebbles, slapping against everything unfortunate enough to lie beneath the tumultuous storm.

It was as if the weather we left back home in Sanguis followed us to Carmina, mocking me with its wickedness and misery.

The hood of my cloak was pulled so far over my head that it felt as if the world had been soaked into a dark grey curtain. Water droplets slid down the cowl toward my nose, and I resisted the urge to fling the useless hood off my face. I gritted my teeth and bore it, knowing hiding our presence was of the utmost importance.

Coming to Carmina was the only option we had to find Astaroth, the son of a bitch who helped kill my family and poison Lo. If any of his cronies got word of our presence, however, I had no doubt he'd go so deep into a hole like the cockroach he was that we'd never find him.

With my luck, that would probably happen, right?

You know—

Don't answer that question, Dev. It's rhetorical, and I'm not in the mood to hear about how this was all fated.

Carmina's dark and brooding clouds loomed over us like a sinister omen. The sky was an inky black canvas, with only one brilliant stroke of lightning illuminating the darkness for a few moments before fading away into oblivion. A crack of thunder caused me to jolt slightly, startled and on edge in this unknown territory. The adrenaline coursing through my veins made me glance around instantly for a threat.

Spitfire, no one is going to hurt you. Even if the gods themselves tried to strike you down right now, I'd kill them before the lightning could ever caress your skin.

Damn it. How did he have the uncanny ability to cut through my shitty moods with kind words? I wasn't sure how he found the words that still somehow touched my heart with how shredded and useless the organ felt in my chest at the moment.

Rain pelted down relentlessly, sending waves of water crashing to the ground and drowning out all other noise in its wake. Our connection was something I was truly grateful for in times like this, where we couldn't physically speak aloud.

Turning to trace my eyes over his lips, that were pulled in a tight line, I shook my head so slightly that I knew he wouldn't actually notice the movement through the rain obscuring even our heightened vision. I was doing my best to not take my god-awful mood out on everyone around me, but my control over it was slipping.

I dare a god to take me on right now, I growled back to him. *I swear there's enough pent-up rage within me to storm Divinus' gates and win.*

That's an interesting thought. Did you know that angels are also given soul weapons?

I didn't ask for a history lesson, Dev, but while we're on the topic, are you saying you couldn't take them on if I followed through with that?

I swear I could *feel* her mental feathers ruffle at my insinuation that she wasn't superior to the weapons of angels, but that's what she gets for butting in on my conversation.

I didn't say that, she huffed, and it felt like a small gap widened between our connection, and I instantly felt like shit.

I was all over the fucking place right now, lashing out unfairly at everyone around me.

The confirmation that a witch was involved in the slaughter of my family wasn't a revelation, but the truth of my best friend's family orchestrating it... I'd been suppressing shit into my deal-with-it-later piles for so long that they were already overflowing. The new piece of information finally pushed me all the way over the damn edge.

My jaw clenched at the memory of the last time I'd seen Jade.

It all felt like I was watching it from an outsider's perspective now, knowing her family's involvement.

"Kill me, Jade," I said, holding my hands wide in a welcoming gesture. Closing my eyes, I felt peace with the knowledge that this was the end.

I waited for her blade to slice into my neck, but as the seconds ticked by, I lost the calm energy I'd found with the acceptance of my inevitable death. Snapping my eyes open, I found Jade staring at me, unmoving.

"Kill me!" I roared, taking a menacing step forward

in an attempt to provoke her.

My eyes clenched shut as I forced my feet forward, stomping through the storm both outside and within my heart.

She didn't even flinch. Instead, she shook her head, her black curls loosely bouncing against her neck as she spared me a glance full of pity. "No. Leave this city, Alina, and never come back."

As I fell to my knees, the dam on my emotions loosened and broke, leaving me wracking with full-bodied sobs. I cried out, my head hanging to allow my silver hair to drape around me like a shield. "Please, Jade. I can't do this. I can't live like this."

There was no warmth to be found in her voice as she spat, "You forgot our most basic rules as slayers. You let your emotions overwhelm you with your mother's death, Alina. You left yourself unprotected in the middle of an attack, and now Skye is dead because of you. Her death has stained your soul, and that is something you must suffer through. I won't put you out of your misery—you don't deserve that kindness."

A small, lifeless laugh fell from my lips.

How could she stand there and cast me out like a rabid animal if she knew it was her family who had done this to me?

Was she a part of it? She was the one who

convinced us to turn off our phones that night. She was the one who somehow knew that no other families were targeted, despite me not having left her side for long.

I'd been a fool, blinded by anguish and pain, and I was played by someone I considered a sister in my heart.

The tips of my nails dug into my palms, eliciting a small gasp as I felt the sting of my skin splitting open and the heat of blood trickling down my skin. I didn't bother trying to hide it from my men, knowing the storm would wash the blood away as my skin healed itself.

We will get justice, Comoroă. I swear it.

Drake's voice grounded me, pulling me back to the present and reminding me that I had bigger fish to fry. As velvety and soothing as his voice could be, it did nothing to sate the rage flowing through me.

Glancing over my shoulder to Lo's covered head —lolling against Drake's shoulder and neck—rage boiled through my veins like a white-hot storm. Desperation crawled up my throat as I thought about the situation we'd found ourselves in.

We needed answers fast, and being unable to use our speed only delayed us further. Every single second mattered when we didn't really know how long Lo had. Despite making the quick decision to have Andrei take his mom back to our castle in Sanguis while Drake, Lincoln, and I traversed the witches' territory, our careful pace only made it feel like we were wasting time.

Drake's eyes clashed with mine, and though they were filled with fear for his sister's life as he spoke in my mind, his words still forced a sense of strength and hope through me that I knew none of us felt.

I know, Comoroă. I know. We're almost there.

Acid filled my tone as I answered, *If we don't get there in—*

Don't. Don't even fucking finish that sentence.

Taking a deep breath, I tried to push all the fury bubbling within me down.

He was right. I couldn't speak the unthinkable into existence. I had to stay strong, just like Lo would if our roles were reversed.

I was barely holding myself together, and I needed to get a grip—quick. As strong as I tried to convince myself I was, all I wanted to do was fall apart and let my tears be swept away alongside the drops of rain whipping at my face until there was an ocean for me to drown in. I couldn't, though. Not yet. I had to stay strong for just a bit longer.

But how long could I convince myself that I was capable of that?

Only time would tell.

Giving him a curt nod of understanding, I turned back around. Step by heart-wrenching step, we walked along the deserted streets until we reached our destination. It felt like a death march, with nothing easing the anxiety and desperation pounding through my skull.

A sense of unease made my skin crawl. It was like we were being watched. The hub of the city was full of vendors and signs of life earlier, but as we neared the mountainous outline of the territory to the north, the number of cities and homes dwindled, along with the energy that came with city life.

Finally, we drew to a halt in front of the home we were set to meet our contact at—well, if you could call it a home. Nothing about it screamed that it was inviting or warm. I definitely wasn't expecting a platter of cookies to be waiting for us inside there. More likely, there was a platter of weapons that they used to kill their enemies.

The imposing structure stood before us, a foreboding presence looming over its decrepit surroundings. The dark-stone exterior of the home was emphasized with ornate carvings of winged creatures perching across the top of the roof, staring down at us like menacing sentinels.

My eyes rested on the statues for a moment, as if they were responsible for the sensation of eyes being focused on me. In a land of magic, I wouldn't put it past the statues to be capable of sentry duty. Letting my gaze fall after seeing no movement, I took in the tall, narrow windows littering the front of the home. Heavy black curtains were drawn shut over them, as if to keep unwanted eyes from prying.

Why the hell are there no guards here if this is such a prominent family? I questioned Drake, knowing he was the only one with information on his contact.

This was where we were supposed to meet them. The Nyx family apparently had a powerful foothold in Carmina, wheeling and dealing in all things whispered in secret. They knew everything, including information that could take Astaroth down. They also happened to be the same family that we hired the Shadow witch, Nimia, from to assist in our interrogation.

You don't need guards when your family is full of some of the most feared witches in Carmina.

A year ago, I would have entirely understood that, thinking that my family was the same as theirs. Who would dare attack us?

An icy feeling of numbness spread through me, and I bit out, *That means nothing. There are always enemies waiting for that one opportune moment.*

I wouldn't let their reputation intimidate me, though. Anyone could be killed, and that meant the Nyx family was just as vulnerable as we were. As I stalked to the door with Lincoln at my side, I felt a shiver run down my spine. The sensation was quickly replaced by relief as the large porch offered shelter from the elements, and the sound of the storm was muted, almost like a spell was cast over the home that allowed us to comfortably lower our sopping wet hoods.

With a jolt, I realized that it probably *was* a spell.

I reached out and grabbed the cold, metal knocker, banging it against the brass plate on the door. As I did, the sound echoed through the halls inside, and we only waited a moment before the door creaked open. A tall, dark figure shrouded in shadows appeared. He was dressed in a black coat that reached his ankles, with dark jeans and a shirt beneath. His hair was slicked back, revealing piercing blue eyes so light they almost appeared white at first glance.

"Welcome," he said coldly, his deep voice exactly

what I imagined it might sound like from just looking at him. "I have been expecting you."

Another shiver crawled up my spine. I swear, that was some typical super-villain shit, delivering a line like that just before someone entered the home they were going to be killed in. But of course, we had no choice but to follow through with this.

His head tilted to the side slightly as his eyes trailed over me slowly, a small smirk putting his dimples on display. But the look disappeared the second our eyes clashed again, his gaze catching on my lengthened fangs as I hissed, "Look at me like that one more time, and I'll make you my next snack. It's been too long since I've fed. Try me, witch."

I wasn't going to ever feed from a human, but he didn't need to know that.

So scary, much wow, Devorare murmured sarcastically, an icy tone accompanying her words.

Yeah, she was definitely mad at me. I deserved it, so I didn't bother quipping back at her.

Instead of backing down like I anticipated, he took a step toward me and flashed me a full smile this time. I swear I saw shadows dancing within the blue of his eyes. "And what makes you think I wouldn't like that, vamp?"

A moment of silence stretched between us before my own smile tugged on my face at the knowledge that it wasn't me he needed to be scared of now.

Lincoln's thoughts were frenzied, pushing into my mind without me even searching for them.

Destroy.

Dismember.

Scorch his existence from this earth.

On cue, Lincoln's hand wrapped around the witch's throat and shoved him into the door frame hard enough to splinter the wood. Lowering his face until he was nose to nose with the witch who kept smiling like his life wasn't in danger, Lincoln growled, "The only reason I haven't ripped your tongue from your throat for speaking to my mate like that is because we still need it for you to tell us a few vital pieces of information. So I suggest you put that mouth to use in the correct manner moving forward."

Yup. That was my man. As possessive and protective as ever. I would be lying if I said the fierceness with which he protected me didn't make my stomach and vagina do cartwheels simultaneously.

A second later, though, a gasp slipped from my

lips as I watched Lincoln suddenly being restrained a few feet off the ground by shadows that curled out of thin air with a snap of the witch's fingers. The shadows forcefully tugged him away from the witch before the little shit stood to his full height and dusted off his chest like vermin had touched him.

My lip curled back in fury.

He looked completely unfazed by Lincoln roughing him up and threatening him. Running a hand through his slicked-back hair, he nodded at Lincoln, who attempted to thrash out of the hold, but to no avail.

I wanted to rush to help him, but I had no damn idea what to do to combat the shadows. My chest tightened with unease. It further proved how over our heads we were in this territory, and I didn't like it one fucking bit.

"I understand and respect your mate bond, but I need you to understand that the only reason I let you do that to me was because I was purposefully testing your group. If I wanted you dead, you would have been before your mate here ever had the chance to knock on my door."

A growl bubbled in my chest at his thinly veiled threat.

Why the fuck did he feel the need to test us? My

hackles raised even further as I narrowed my eyes on the witch.

Silence descended as he snapped his fingers. The shadows vanished from Lincoln's body, dropping him back to his feet to my left. My eyes lingered on him for a moment to ensure he was okay, waiting for him to straighten and give me a nod.

A heavy sigh came from Drake as he pushed forward on my right. I recognized his sigh as one of pure exhaustion, and I completely understood. The night had come and gone as we traveled, and we were all running on fumes and desperation.

"Alexi, may we please come in? Oleander is expecting us, and as you can see, my sister is in dire condition."

Of course, Drake knew this guy's name. Why couldn't he have said that earlier?

Alexi's head swung to Drake and Lo before sweeping his arm toward the door with a saccharine smile. "Please, make yourself at home, Dracula. It's our family's honor to assist you once more. I must ask, however, did our contact relay to you that the payment this time is different from what was asked for with the use of our Shadow witch, Nimia?"

What the fuck did that mean?

Dread pooled in my stomach. I didn't like

unknown variables, and they were somehow begin-ning to stack up by the minute.

My eyes darted to Drake, noting that he was barely concealing his annoyance, a minor tick in his jaw the only indication of his true feelings. He was the polite and well-put-together one of our group, always maintaining decorum for the sake of getting resolutions to our problems when the rest of us were too reactionary with our emotions. Though with Lo's life on the line, I wasn't sure how much longer he could pull it off. This Alexi fellow was playing with fire. I, for one, would love to see him get burned.

"And what's the expected payment now?" he gritted out between clenched teeth as he raised a dark eyebrow.

The black veins below his eyes appeared, and I knew he was dangerously close to losing his grip on not only his polite persona but on his control of the monster within him as well.

I couldn't deny that I wanted to see it unleashed one day. But today wasn't the day.

The slimy witch's eyes slid to me, making my skin crawl with his attention as he rumbled, "Let's call it an 'IOU' from your little mate."

CHAPTER TWO
ALINA

The little shit really had it coming. Those words elicited strong reactions from both Drake and Lincoln, who hissed and bared their fangs as they took menacing steps forward. However, I had already seen how quickly we could get into a shitty predicament with Alexi's power, so I held out my hands, gesturing for them to stop. Shockingly, they did, which proved to me that they *did* understand restraint. So they just *chose* not to practice it, I realized with gritted teeth. Taking a deep breath, I reminded myself that we were all working on that.

Just the thought of how my men reacted had me aching for Andrei to be with us. Despite being the youngest of my mates, he was somehow the most grounded and neutral when it came to charged situations. I loved that about him but hated that his ability to compartmentalize each moment stemmed from having to keep his emotions and reactions under control because of his abusive father.

I had to stop myself from lingering on thoughts of how he and his mom were doing back home and focus on the moment at hand instead.

I took a large step forward, then another, and I didn't stop until I was staring up into the witch's icy eyes. It didn't escape me that they perfectly matched the ice block he'd proven was in his chest instead of his heart. I rubbed at my chin, offering a look like I was deep in thought. My brow pinched as I held up a finger and exclaimed, "I've got it! The only favor you'd ever get from me would be removing the broomstick that's lodged up your puckered asshole."

I plastered on a beaming smile as I crossed my arms in satisfaction, seeing the way a storm brewed in his darkening eyes.

Just because we needed help from them didn't mean I was going to allow us to be treated like shit. I was of the mindset that as long as you set your boundaries with someone early on, they'd stop trying to push you when they realized they couldn't achieve their desired outcome. Typical bully tactics.

"Alexi, stop this at once!"

The sharp command was sudden and loud, and it felt as if it echoed through the house on a stereo system. Wincing as my eardrums rang, I wished for once that we didn't have heightened senses.

I mean, really, all someone had to do was bang a gong around a vampire army, and they'd be on their knees. Seemed like a pretty big genetic flaw in the evolution of vampires if we were supposed to be the big, bad predators.

As the pain receded, I was able to fully focus on the new man who came into view next to Alexi. Alexi suddenly looked like a scolded child, not the imposing witch who had wrapped Lincoln up in his shadows moments before.

Funny how things changed drastically when the thing above you in the hierarchy appeared.

The new witch was the opposite of Alexi, with deep brown eyes and black hair that had a purple hue in the darkness. Almost like a raven's feather. He was dressed a hell of a lot nicer than Alexi, too. Dark-navy slacks adorned his long legs, paired with a pressed white dress shirt and a shiny black belt. His dress shoes sparkled in the dim light, making it look like his favorite pastime was shining them.

What a sad life they must live out here in this deserted territory.

"Oleander," Drake rumbled in greeting, though there was a considerable lack of warmth in his words. "What did your associate mean when he stated that the terms of payment have changed?"

All of our eyes locked onto Oleander as Alexi faded away inside the house along with the shadows, leaving us with who I was assuming was our actual point of contact. But Oleander's gaze wasn't fixed on any of us who were currently staring daggers at him; it was on Lo, his eyes glued to her face as she let out the softest moan of pain from Drake's back.

My heart rate spiked in response to the soft, keening noise. She'd been as quiet as a mouse for the better part of our journey, but as time passed, the pain she was suffering internally became more evident.

As a slayer, I'd been taught that the only way to kill a vampire was by beheading. I was learning that wasn't true. Besides being in possession of a weapon that could smite vampires, I also now knew that whatever she'd been dosed with was supposed to be the slowest, most painful death a vampire could face. Her sounds marked a downturn in her condition, no matter how faint they were now. My stomach churned, knowing that the pain would only get worse.

The witch's dark brows furrowed before his gaze bounced between all of our faces, confusion dancing in his eyes. Landing on Drake in the end, he demanded, "Tell me what is wrong with her. Now."

My mouth dropped open in shock as white-hot heat seared through my veins, bubbling beneath the surface of my skin. Who the hell did he think he was?

Lincoln stepped forward to cut off his view of Lo, taking a protective stance before retorting, "We don't owe you any information. We're the ones who are here to collect information from you. So stop wasting our time. Your little lap dog has done enough of that since we stepped foot on this property."

Well said, love.

I'm so fucking fed up with these witches.

I couldn't agree more. It was apparent that Alexi wasn't as important as he'd made himself seem at first, and that knowledge made me want to hold the edge of Devorare's blade to his neck until he begged for forgiveness for wasting what time Lo had left.

"As you can see, we don't have time to waste,"

Drake said, echoing my thoughts. His tone was much kinder, which seemed to appease the pinch of annoyance Oleander took on from Lincoln's words.

Being polite and pleasant wasn't my strong suit, and these witches were being such fucking pricks. They deserved all the attitude we were giving them. Drake was a saint for attempting even the tiniest amount of niceties and decorum.

Pulling on the edges of the crisp cuffs of his dress shirt, as if standing out here had wrinkled the impeccably pressed material, Oleander gave a sharp nod before gesturing inside. The way he glanced at his watch as if we were the ones wasting time grated on my nerves. "Please, come in. We do have a lot to discuss."

I barely held in the scoff that threatened to escape me. Last time I checked, they were the ones dicking around.

Stepping inside, we were quickly ushered down a long, narrow hall that was completely devoid of personal touches other than black paisley-patterned wallpaper. I couldn't help but glance warily at all the closed doors on either side of us as we walked, as if someone was going to pop out of one to attack us at any moment.

Thankfully, we made it to the end of the hall

quickly, alleviating my fears. These guys might be assholes, but I didn't think Drake would take us somewhere he expected us to be attacked.

I took in the room that opened up before us with an impressed nod. *This* was what I expected from a Gothic home.

We stepped into the large sitting room, complete with not one but two burning fireplaces on opposing sides of the room. A fluffy, dark-grey rug sprawled throughout the majority of the space. A luxurious velvet couch sat on the far side of a shiny glass-topped coffee table, flanked on the opposite ends by two oversized chairs. Above it all hung a massive black chandelier that glittered with the light from the flames roaring in the fireplaces.

The wallpaper was different in here, giving off the barest hint of a deep, blood-red tint that made my stomach growl. My eyes went wide in embarrassment. It really had been too long since we'd fed, and I made a mental note to keep an eye out for an animal, *any animal,* on the last leg of our journey. No part of me wanted to feed directly from a *living* being, even if it was an animal, but it was better than losing control and going on a rampage when I let my hunger grow past my limits.

We'll find you something, Comoroă. Don't

worry. We just need to quickly get this information, and then we'll be on our way.

Drake's words eased my momentary panic as I sank down onto the plush couch next to him, easing Lo's head onto my legs as he situated her to lie across us. As I glanced down at her, her eyebrows drew together, and her eyes pinched at the corners. A ragged puff of air fell from her lips, and I couldn't help but run my fingers across her cheek, wishing I could pull all of her pain out of her and into myself.

I could say with the utmost certainty that she was one of the most pure souls I'd ever met. I would bet my life that there weren't many people in all of Praeditus, Ordinarius, Divinus, and Hell combined that would sacrifice their lives to ensure their loved ones didn't have to deal with the guilt of that choice, like she had.

If—I mean, *when*—we got her back, she was absolutely going to get an earful from me about her actions. I swear, this shit was taking years off my *supposed* immortal life. But dammit, I couldn't even really be mad at her for making such a selfless, albeit reckless, move.

That was our Lo—the radiant sunshine that made the darkest days brighter with her caring heart.

As Lincoln settled into the oversized chair to my left, Oleander paced in front of the table for a few seconds before coming to a halt. Dragging my eyes up, I found him completely enraptured by Lo once more.

My blood boiled as my heart began to hammer in my chest again.

Why the fuck did he keep staring at her? She wasn't some science experiment to gawk at.

My fangs slipped out of their own accord, and I bared them at him, hissing, "Do you think her corpse will be as beautiful to stare at? Because that's all we're going to have left if you don't start fucking talking."

Calm yourself, Comoroă. He isn't looking at her in an aggressive manner. It is troubling in an entirely different way, however.

Confusion clouded my brain at Drake's words, making my fangs retract. As I watched Oleander tear his eyes away from her, I noted the strain it took for him to do so. His throat bobbed as he swallowed hard, nostrils flaring as he drew a deep breath.

There was a tick in his jaw as I watched it clench and unclench over and over again. After a long moment, he finally cleared his throat and spoke. "I do apologize for Alexi's earlier behavior. He is stationed here for his training. Unfortunately, we don't get many visitors, and he was poking at you for his own amusement. He will be reprimanded for his actions."

My chin lifted slightly in silent victory as I let out a huff of air from my nose. *Fuck Alexi.*

Oleander's arms lifted to cross against his chest, the material straining from the muscles bunching beneath as his eyes drifted to Lo once more. I resisted the natural urge to shield her from sight with my body as he continued, "I know you are here for information on Astaroth, but I want to ask if you'll allow me to inspect her. I can feel the magic inside of her, and I'd like to see if there is something I can do to relieve her pain in the meantime—even if I can't cure her."

There was magic inside of her? Fuck, that made this a hell of a lot more complicated. I'd been assuming that we were just dealing with a simple poison. The antidote Serena had been given had to be more than I'd initially thought.

My eyes swung back and forth from Oleander's strained face to Drake's pensive one, knowing I'd go with whatever my mate's response was. While I loved Lo fiercely, he got the final say here.

Everything in me screamed that Oleander could

make Lo's condition worse with whatever he wanted to do, and there was nothing we'd be able to do about it. Despite trying to learn how to master my emotions, they still ruled my judgment, and I didn't trust anyone outside our fucked-up rhombus of a group, as Lincoln called us.

Damn right, Princess. It's us against the world.

Us. The way he spoke the word with such conviction into my head was the lifeline I needed to remind myself that even when things seem impossible, they could still work out. I once thought there was no way I could find a way for my mates to coexist in the same room without beating each other to a pulp, but they'd exceeded my expectations. We had finally found a way to fit all of our jagged pieces together into a beautiful puzzle that wouldn't make sense to anyone outside of us.

We'd find a way to beat these odds, too.

Drake shifted on my right, and I felt unease rolling off him in waves, which really set my nerves on high alert. The intense, fearsome Dracula... uneasy? Fuck.

He finally relented. "You may try, but I'm warning you, Oleander—" His voice deepened, the rough tone sounding strained as he continued, "If you hurt her, I do not have the control within me to stop myself from killing you. Is it worth your life to you to risk that?"

Drake's specific choice of words set my mind spinning, and I felt my face screwing up in contemplation. Was it worth it to Oleander to risk his life? Of course it wasn't. Lo was a stranger to him. Someone who hadn't even uttered a single word to him, yet Drake was asking him if he would risk his life for even a possibility of easing her suffering.

Peculiar.

I was willing to be hated for you for the rest of our lives as long as I was able to protect you, Comoroă. The things we do for our fated can't be explained.

I couldn't stop my face from whipping toward him at the implication.

Are you saying that you think they have a mate bond, Drake?

CHAPTER THREE
ALINA

Drake's silence was answer enough, and I was left gaping at him, blinking furiously as I processed the possibility.

No fucking way. We were only here to ensure that we got the answers we needed to help Lo, not to add this insane possibility to her plate for when she wakes up.

What were the odds? They were two different species from entirely different worlds. Would they have ever found their way to each other if this hadn't happened to Lo at the hands of the vampire she had chosen for herself?

Are you starting to believe me about fate now, Alina?

A groan wormed its way from my throat,

drawing the eyes of Lincoln and Drake. I waved them off, muttering, "It's just Dev talking."

Yeah, you're right, it is me talking. And once again, it's you not listening, Alina.

The sass levels were reaching an all-time high with her. I didn't think that was possible, and I fought against the instinctual reaction of letting the attitude grate on my nerves.

Think about what you just thought. Lo would have never met her mate, if that's what they are, if everything in your life hadn't happened exactly the way it did. She had to go through this awful situation to be here. Maybe that doesn't seem fair, but in the end, does it lead to a happier life for her with him at her side?

Dev leapt ten steps ahead just to try to prove this never-ending point of hers about *fate* that had become a permanent thorn in my side. I didn't think I would ever really understand why it mattered so much to her that I gave into this fate and destiny shit that she put so much stock in.

Let's not get ahead of ourselves here, Dev. None of it matters if she doesn't survive. What if she doesn't? Then what? Does her supposed mate get to live with heartbreak for the rest of his life? Sounds really fair of fate.

As if on cue, Lo cried out and thrashed in our

laps, almost punching me in the face, but I just managed to lean back in time. The very tips of her knuckles brushed against my jaw, and even that hint of contact had me jolting.

Girl had a mean right hook.

Instantly, Drake and I secured her arms and legs, using our body weight to trap her and prevent her from hurting herself or anyone else. Oleander came to kneel in front of me as I grunted at the force of her thrashing in my arms. He shoved the coffee table to the side like it weighed half a pound to get close to her.

He hesitated for a moment, but I couldn't decipher if it was from confusion or doubt.

"It's worth it," he said so quietly that I wasn't immediately sure if he was trying to convince us or himself of it.

Indecision plagued my gut alongside the bile I felt churning in there. If this went sideways, I'd never be able to live with myself. My eyes widened as all the potentially horrible outcomes hurtled into my brain. My hair whipped around my face as I jerked my head at Drake. I needed him to center my unraveling thoughts before I did something rash.

Are you sure we can trust him, Drake?

His jaw ticked before he met my eyes. They were

still the obsidian black depths he wore around strangers, but the black veins beneath his eyes had traveled all the way to his cheeks now.

He was struggling just as much as me, if not more.

No, I'm not, Comoroă. But sometimes we have to take a leap of faith, no matter how daunting it feels. Look at him right now, and I mean really look at him. Do you get any sense of malicious intent?

I did as he instructed, forcing myself to take deep, calming breaths to clear my frantic brain enough to focus. Oleander's fingers trembled as he reached toward Lo, brushing away the loose curls that had fallen over her face as she thrashed around, and gently tucked them behind her ear.

If you do feel anything, I will tell him to stop right now. But don't give me an answer based solely on your fear of the worst possible outcomes.

The reverence I saw in Oleander's face, his mouth popping open with the shallowest inhale of breath as their skin connected, felt so...pure. As his hand slid down to cup her cheek firmly, there was a note of anguish in his eyes. The way he stared at her alone absolutely had me considering the mate bond theory, but what solidified it in my mind was the way Lo instantly stilled at his touch. As if it brought her immense peace to just feel him, despite not being conscious enough to even know who was touching her.

Did her soul sense it?

Drake and I warily relaxed our grips on her and sat back against the couch, waiting to see if she would start thrashing again.

The faintest ghost of a smile tugged Oleander's lips up at the corners. I thought that if I could read his mind right now, it would be filled with thoughts of sheer joy and validation that what he was feeling wasn't one-sided. No matter how crazy it was.

I have to trust that. I have to.

It was the exact same way I felt when my mates surrounded me with their presence and touch. Well, when they weren't pissing me off, but even when they were, everything still seemed... better with their presence. I felt supported and loved. Complete, even. It was a connection that was too hard to describe. How did you describe such a love with mere words? It was impossible. Unexplainable. Yet here it was, right in front of my eyes.

Are they...? Lincoln asked in confusion as I felt the weight of his stare heavily on the side of my face.

He didn't need to finish the question. It was so obvious now.

I inhaled deeply, feeling a bit of whiplash at the sudden turn of events.

Yup, I think so.

I'd never heard of cross-species mate bonds, but I guess that didn't mean shit with how little I apparently knew about the world around us. Their bond brought up so many questions—many of them ones that I didn't want the answers to. Like, what would they do if they *were* mates? Would Lo leave our territory to come here? Would he come to Sanguis? Would they even accept their bond and work past their differences?

Watching the adoration in Oleander's eyes as they scanned Lo's face, like he was soaking in every little detail of her beauty, made that point of pain twist deeper within me. I wanted her to be treasured and loved in the way she deserved, but I wanted it to happen at our sides.

Did that make me a selfish asshole? Probably, but I'd already lost my family. I didn't want to lose her too.

I wasn't ready to face the reality that she might someday leave us for her mate. If we got to that point, I knew I'd be grateful in the end because it meant that Lo continued to live and find what I hoped was a true, deep love. Not the shallow, narcissistic love Rin had given her.

I still owed that little shit a beat down for his hand in all of this. The way he tucked tail and ran, knowing she was dying, only proved how undeserving he was of her. He'd never loved her.

Oleander's eyes closed as his head bent forward, as if in silent prayer, as he pressed his hand firmly to her cheek. Shadows began to pour from his hand, and I fought to keep from squirming as they grew, wrapping around Lo in an intimate embrace.

If I hadn't been around a Shadow witch recently and seen the way their magic worked, I would have jumped off the couch and taken Lo far, far away. No matter if I thought they could be mates or not. As it was, I felt a touch of pride in myself for not letting out the squeak that pushed its way up my throat as the tendrils tickled against my arms.

The words that Nimia uttered to me just the day before rolled through my brain.

"They're just saying hello, Alina."

I know she meant for that to be a soothing concept, but honestly, the thought of the shadows being an entity that wanted to interact with me only made it that much creepier.

Oleander interrupted my minor panic attack at the feeling of one of his shadows crawling up my chest—perverted little shadow. What is it saying hi to, my tits? Not that they weren't worthy of the attention, but they were spoken for—thrice over.

"My shadows help me detect magic, no matter the kind. Within our world, there is Blood, Shadow, Lunar, and..." He trailed off, a note of hesitance in his voice as he stared at Lo reverently. My stomach twisted, but my interest was piqued. After a quiet moment, he finally murmured, "Unblessed."

Damn me for not learning more about witches in school before coming here.

Before I could ask him what Unblessed witches were, he let out a grunt, his face etched with pain from the exertion of his magic, it seemed. "Whatever she's been injected with is a mix of Shadow and Blood magic. It's a nasty combination, and it seems like whatever she was given was a very high-level potion. It takes an extremely delicate touch to weave them together like this."

Her body began to shake, her mouth falling open in a silent scream. I moved to shove him off her, my knee-jerk reaction being to rip her away from what was hurting her, but his eyes snapped up to mine.

He steeled his shoulders, his eyes flashing as if he would fight me if needed.

His voice was clipped as he said, "I can coax out the Shadow portion from her. It won't be comfortable, but it will alleviate some of the pain she's facing. You have to let me do this, Alina."

Of course, it wasn't going to be simple or painless. We'd never be so lucky to find someone who could actually fix our problem quickly. Fate didn't like to work in our favor like that.

I forced myself to breathe through the frantic anxiety pulsing through me. Chewing the inside of my cheek, I forced a nod at Oleander, showing that I wasn't going to stop him.

Tendrils of smoke began to stream from her gaping mouth, painting the ceiling with shadows. My eyes bulged—it looked like she was being fucking exorcised and the evil that was pouring out of her had nowhere to go.

Lincoln and I shared a look of uncertainty before we turned our gazes up, where it continued to pool across the ceiling.

Finally, she stopped shaking, and her mouth closed, seemingly free of the dark matter for now.

My shoulders sagged, and I took a deep breath of relief. It'd actually worked.

A part of me willed her eyes to open, hoping that she would be cured enough for us to see a glimpse of those beautiful eyes and reassure us that she was going to be okay. Wishing that she could hang on for longer now. But all she did was nuzzle into Oleander's hand as she let out a heavy sigh, seeking comfort in her unconscious state from a man she didn't know.

It was enough of a positive to let the knot in my throat loosen, allowing me to breathe a little easier with the hope she wasn't as close to the edge of death as she had been.

"What the fuck just happened?" I finally asked, glancing at Drake, half expecting him to know with his expansive knowledge of the machinations of the world.

I was met with a silent shrug as his brow furrowed in concentration, almost like he could find the answers buried somewhere deep in his brain if he tried hard enough.

Oleander's hand slipped away from Lo's face as he rocked back to sit on his heels in front of the couch. But his focus was still completely on her as he spoke to us. "Whatever is in her system is attacking her heart. The shadows were wrapped around it in a vice-like grip to prevent anything from interfering with the Blood magic pumping within the organ. It's just the first layer of the problem, however."

What. The. Fuck.

Her writhing started back up, but it didn't seem like it was coming from a place of pain, more like a sense of searching. Her body jerked towards Oleander, and if Drake and I hadn't instantly pinned her down, she would have fallen straight off the couch.

Was she seeking out his touch again? I wasn't sure if my heart broke at the move or if it was already broken and being put back together. Too much was happening at once to let me fully process that this was really happening between them.

I watched as Oleander sucked in a breath and bit his lip hard, his hands on his thighs curling into tight fists like he was resisting the urge to rip her from our laps.

I glanced at Drake, nibbling on my lip in thought. *If his touch eases her pain and brings her comfort, I think we should let him hold her.*

Drake let out a grunt with a subtle shake of his head, like he couldn't believe he actually agreed with me. Or maybe it was downright bewilderment over the fact that this was the situation we were faced with in the first place—because same.

In unison, we lifted her gently off our laps. Oleander's entire face lit up as he stretched his arms to gather her reverently into his embrace. Instantly, she curled against his chest and nuzzled into his neck, earning a tender smile from Oleander.

It was so damn cute that I actually grinned, despite knowing how precarious her situation still was. Hell, it was renewing my belief that we would get this cure. Determination filled me—I wanted her to experience this for real. It didn't matter if it took her away from our lives a bit. She deserved this.

As he settled into the chair to the right of Drake, situating her until she rested easily against him, he glanced up at us. Finally, he looked like he could tear his eyes away from her without being in pain. His hand on her back traced circles continuously as he asked, "Can you please tell me how this happened to her? It's important to me, as you can probably decipher."

Drake spoke first, and I vowed to follow his lead on how much he was willing to share with the witch. Just because Oleander was potentially Lo's mate didn't mean he was suddenly a trusted ally. We were in unknown territory and needed to tread carefully.

"We were fighting enemies in our own territory,

and an unfortunate situation led to two of our people being injected with whatever..." he said, gesturing toward Lo, "this is. When we were able to pin down the one vial of the antidote that was on the premises, we had a brief conversation about who would receive it."

My heart squeezed as visions of the very recent memory filled my mind. There was only one other time in my life that I'd felt so fucking helpless and lost. I would have given anything in that moment—just like when I found my family slaughtered—to change it all, but I couldn't.

"She took the decision away from us," I whispered softly, a slight tremble in my voice. Emotion clogged my throat, making it hard to swallow as I dragged my gaze, which had fallen to the ground, back up to meet Oleander's. I wanted him to realize what a fucking treasure he had in his arms. "She mustered the energy to force the vial down the throat of the other victim. She said she couldn't live with the guilt of leaving such an awful decision to the people she loved."

When I didn't carry on, too choked up to breathe properly, Lincoln added, "She's one of the kindest and most selfless people I've had the honor of meeting in my many years of life."

Drake's heavy emotions slammed into me, and I squeezed myself closer to his side, leaning my head onto his shoulder. I couldn't take away his overwhelming fear of losing her, but I could show him that I was here for every second of this. I took his hand in mine, laying it on top of his thigh with a gentle caress over his knuckles to provide him silent support.

His body shook slightly as he choked out, "Before I found my mate, Lo was the reason I pushed on for so many miserable fucking years. She was a little shit at times, but she's always been *my* little shit of a sister." He took a moment, swallowing thickly as his voice pitched up, breaking from the emotion clogging his throat. "She is so picky with who she gives her love to, but when she does, it's the greatest gift in the world."

"If I'm ever lucky enough to receive that gift," Oleander started as he gazed down at Lo, pulling her just a little bit closer to him before continuing, "I swear to you that I will ensure I give the exact same thing back to her." His eyes drifted away from her face long enough to lock with Drake's. "She will want for nothing."

Suddenly, I had the feeling of being at a wedding and watching a father give his daughter away at the altar. The air around us felt supercharged with emotion. The intense energy that crackled in the air was the kind that I knew would last in my memories for the rest of my life. It was a monumental moment, one that I could say with absolute certainty that not a single person in this room expected to happen at this meeting.

When Drake gave a final nod of approval, it felt like I could breathe again. My first sharp inhale seemed to break the spell of emotion washing over our small group, and everyone's focus seemed to shift and snap into strategy mode.

"You need to get to the mountain behind this home. Now," Oleander stated, glancing between the three of us. "One of Astaroth's residences is located there, and I know for a fact that he isn't currently there. It's the perfect time to bargain with the witch, that is."

The suspicious part of me couldn't help but wonder why he knew that. It was my natural reaction to distrust until someone proved themselves to me, and I knew that. I had to shake off the bad habit as a new issue slammed into the forefront of my brain.

"Then how the fuck are we supposed to get the

antidote?" I asked, sitting up with the fear that straightened my spine like an iron rod.

Astaroth was our only chance. Who else would know the antidote? He'd supposedly been the one to make it, and at such a high skill level, where would we find someone else who would know?

Oleander's short hair tossed around softly as he shook his head. He raised an eyebrow at me, pinning me with a serious look before answering, "His second in command at this base is always there. He's a seedy bastard, and if you trade him something he finds valuable, he'll give you the antidote. Witches like them have no loyalty to anyone other than themselves."

Lincoln shifted, leaning forward in his chair, his eyes narrowing. "Who is his second, and what would he find of value?"

A cold chuckle escaped Oleander. I couldn't say I liked the sound of it, given our situation.

"You have one thing in common with him—your love of blood. He's a Blood witch. He might want blood from one of you."

My eyebrows rose at the admission. Momentarily, relief washed through me. Well, that wasn't that bad, right? We'd just fill ourselves back up with a feeding after we got the antidote.

"What's the catch?" Drake quickly asked, distrust coloring his tone.

Oleander's nostrils flared as he took a deep breath, holding it for a moment before blowing it out. Something akin to pity entered his eyes as he said, "A Blood witch that is at the height of their power can use the blood of their victims to control them, no matter how far they are. Blood manipulation."

Well, shit.

CHAPTER FOUR
DRAKE

My teeth ground together at Oleander's admission, my eyes snapping to Lincoln over Alina's head. We had to be united in how we chose to move forward from here.

This simply couldn't happen. It was the worst-case scenario we could have asked for.

Alina would risk anything for those she loved, just like Lo would. It's why I loved them both so much. Simultaneously, it was the same reason they both drove me crazy. They would lie, kill, and do anything necessary to protect what was theirs, which made them unpredictable.

You know she would offer her blood for Lo, consequences be damned. We need a plan, Lincoln.

His hands clasped together between his knees as he rested his forearms on his thighs, sighing heavily. I understood the exhaustion painted in his bleary eyes. It felt like we'd been going nonstop. Between learning how to fit into each other's lives with Alina central to our core group, the attempted coup by my board members, trying to help Alina get justice for her family's deaths, and now having Lo's life hanging in the balance, rest wasn't easy to come by. Now it seemed damn near impossible.

What I wouldn't give to have it all fixed with a snap of my fingers. The pressure bearing down on us seemed never-ending, and I could feel all of our patience and optimism waning with each day that passed, each somehow more chaotic than the last.

The veins running up Lincoln's forearms pulsed as he squeezed his hands tight together. His tone was gruff as he responded, *Yeah, I know. So what are we going to offer him that's more valuable to a Blood witch than what he really wants? None of us can risk giving him our blood.*

The truth was, I didn't know.

It was eating me up inside that he and Alina had been looking to me for answers on the witches' powers since coming to this territory, and I wasn't able to provide them. Of course, they expected me to know. I was the oldest living vampire *and* the king of my own territory. I should have been more prepared.

I felt like a failure at a time when my family needed me most, which was making it unbearably hard to keep the beast within me chained away. I wanted to let the shackles fall off and let it out.

It wanted to raze everything to the ground, with no regard for this territory or those who resided in it. The beast wouldn't rest until we had the antidote and our mate back in my bed, stuffed full of our cock.

Can you put a wall back up between us if that's the route your brain's going to go down? I'm trying to focus here, not get an erection from Hell that's going to give me blue balls thinking about Alina's naked body writhing on my cock.

Surprisingly, his tone wasn't one of jealousy or arrogance. It certainly didn't feel like he was upset with me for my lewd thoughts about our mate, and I had to admit that it was thrilling. Sharing Alina in the shower was something I wanted to do over and over again. She'd been a shaking mess with the sensation of having more than one of us involved, and anything that made her legs weak was something I intended to repeat.

Oblivious to our completely inappropriate

conversation, Alina piped up, still focused on Oleander and Lo, "But how do we know he will actually know the antidote if he isn't the witch that brewed it?"

How about we agree to put a pin in that particular thought for now until we get back home?

My words were said with intention, meant to gauge where Lincoln was at with accepting our mutual bond. Our mate was strong and willful, and she belonged with all of us at home. And I clearly meant the castle in our mountains as home, but was his home still at DIA?

His eyes narrowed on me, letting the silence stretch between us as he mulled the question over before shifting his gaze to our mate.

Oleander prattled on in response to Alina as I practically stared a hole in the side of Lincoln's face. He continued to look at Alina, seemingly in deep thought over my question.

"Being a high-level Blood witch, he will be able to provide it. It is likely he had a hand in brewing it, and Astaroth likely provided the finishing touches on it with the Shadow part."

His words were as cold as a bucket of ice water poured over me—an easy reminder of how lacking I was going into this dangerous situation. It was my responsibility to ensure we all got home safely, but I didn't have the tools to do that.

My monster's nails threatened to burst through the tips of my fingers at that truth. I had to dig them into my thighs and count back from five while taking deep breaths to put that anger back inside its box.

If these witches attacked us, which was highly likely, what the fuck were we going to do? Could our speed, strength, and fast reflexes be enough?

While I did have a general knowledge of the political structure of each territory—on the off chance that I needed to interact with the leaders of each grouping—I was kicking myself for not spending more time learning the power details of them. I'd had ample time but had focused all of my efforts on building my own territory and establishing a culture that could survive and thrive.

It'd been foolish of me to be so laser-focused, and now I was paying the price. How could I call myself a king or an effective leader without knowing the extent of our enemies' strengths? First, I'd let the wool be pulled over my eyes by my own board, by people I'd foolishly wanted to trust implicitly.

Stop your fucking pity party, Lincoln scoffed at me mentally. ***We're all adults here and responsible***

for our own safety. Agonizing over what you don't know will only be detrimental to the situation at hand if it's distracting you. Shut up in that head of yours and ask questions if you want answers you don't have.

His bluntness shocked me, my eyes widening at the almost-crass tone he'd taken with me. Somehow, it was exactly what I needed to hear for my monster to fully rest in my chest. The callout pushed the rising panic away, allowing me the space to feel like I had a way to wrest control back instead of feeling weak and unable to provide. Lincoln was right. I could seek answers now, even if it was last minute.

I slumped back in my seat, my shoulders relaxing. No one ever talked to me like that, besides Alina and Lo, of course. The fact that I hadn't felt the visceral urge to rip his throat out over it was huge.

I offered him a small incline of my head, agreeing with his assessment.

His words were wise, and I respected him for being bold enough to tell me the hard truth when I needed to hear it. Especially when our history wasn't the smoothest.

Boldness was a trait I admired in people when it came from a place of good intentions. None of us were perfect, and we needed people around us who were going to push us to be better. While I'd certainly never pictured having to share my mate with anyone, let alone *two* others, I was warming up to it a hell of a lot quicker than I thought I would.

And to answer your previous question, he said, changing the topic quickly and piquing my interest as he leaned back in his chair and glanced lovingly at Alina. ***We won't be home until we build Alina the dream house she wants. I've spoken to her about it briefly. She wants a place that is truly all of ours. That means starting over somewhere together.***

While I could easily picture my castle as our home for the rest of time, I understood Alina's desire for a fresh start. She and her other bonds wouldn't be able to picture it as theirs because it was always going to be mine in their eyes.

Perhaps I could leave the castle to Lo or turn it into an event center for Sanguis. I enjoyed the seclusion and views it afforded us, but I had no real emotional attachment to it. I'd travel to wherever my treasure wanted to be.

Done. When Lo has healed and the situation with the slayers is handled, giving Alina the home she deserves will be our priority.

I'd stopped listening to Alina and Oleander

during my momentary pity party, but the witch's next words caught my attention.

"You must use your speed. I understand why you haven't been using it in order to avoid detection to this point, but we have no idea how long she has," he whispered, a frantic look in his wide eyes as he looked down at Lo. "I may have pulled a portion of the magic out of her, but I am not skilled in Blood magic. I have no way to check that, so I can only guess at the damage it's doing to her."

The urgency and fear in his tone snapped me back to reality, and I pushed to my feet. The exhaustion pulling at my mind made it too easy to slip into mental tangents. Alina and Lincoln quickly followed suit, standing up. I stared down intently at Lo, noting the way her brow furrowed despite being in Oleander's embrace.

He was right. We couldn't rely on whatever he'd done to ease the suffering the spell inflicted on her body. Everything in me wanted to fight the words that fell from my lips next.

"This will probably be far too dangerous to risk having Lo with us. We need to move fast, and if there is a fight, we can't risk her being hurt further. Or being used by them to distract us."

My stomach twisted with the knowledge that I

had to leave my most trusted confidant, my sister in all but blood, here with a witch I would have never trusted for anything other than the information he had for trade before today. My family is in the hands of a stranger.

I must have been projecting my insecurities over the matter loudly because Alina's fingers came to rest on the inside of my bicep, squeezing lightly. Through this tragedy, I somehow managed to fall even harder for my mate. For such a headstrong woman who loved to be in control, she'd taken a step back and followed my lead, allowing me to make all the decisions pertaining to Lo. Every moment, she showed she had my back and supported whatever I chose in the small ways that she could.

I knew her love for Lo had grown tremendously throughout their short time together, and it wasn't lost on me that she was trusting me to get our girl through this.

I couldn't fail my family. I *wouldn't* fail my family.

Oleander nodded in agreement, his hold on her tightening. "Leave her with me, and I will protect her to my dying breath. She is safe in this home." He paused for a moment, his head tilting to the side as my lips pulled into a flat line. "I know those words mean nothing to you, as we do not have a rapport. Trust that in the Nyx family we protect our own, and Lo is now one of our own."

Part of the Nyx family—I knew eventually I'd have to let her go to live her life with whoever she chose, but it had been us against the world for so long that it fucking hurt to hear her being considered a part of someone else's family.

His pretty words meant nothing to me without the action to back them up, but I had no choice but to trust my gut and believe he meant them. I was going entirely off the feeling I got when I saw Oleander and Lo together, which was saying a lot since she was unconscious. I wished she would wake up long enough for me to confirm that she felt the bond to Oleander just as he did, but we didn't have that luxury. Time couldn't be spared to wait, so blind trust it was, as unusual as that was for me.

I let the inky darkness of my monster come out enough to elongate my fingers into black tips, feeling the burning beneath my eyes that signaled the spread there. I knew it was an intimidating look to many, but Oleander simply stared me in the eyes, unwavering in his stance. It put my nerves slightly at ease to see him not cower at the display. It inspired hope in me that he wasn't afraid of my retribution because he would simply hold true to his word.

"You know what I will do if something happens to her, so I won't bother recounting the bloody details to you," I muttered, pulling the beast back. "We need a map marking the location, human and animal blood, and any information you can provide on what to watch for that would indicate an attack from them with us being unaware of their powers."

With a snap of his fingers, Oleander summoned Alexi. A swirl of shadows appeared before the solid form of the younger witch stepped through them.

Ahh, perfect timing.

Now that I didn't have Lo on my back—and knew Oleander had a vested interest in us as Lo's family—there was nothing holding me back from ensuring Alexi knew I wouldn't tolerate his insufferable attitude and disrespect any further.

I need to handle something quickly, Comoroă, I rushed to say in her mind as I pulled her hand off my bicep and gently brushed my lips over her knuckles.

Before Alexi could ask Oleander what he needed, I had him pinned to the floor, right out of reach of the roaring flame in the fireplace. Making quick work of snapping each of his fingers in quick succession, after noting that was how he'd called his shadows forward with Lincoln.

I let out an exhausted sigh.

Clearly, he'd never experienced true pain, screaming as he was. A few broken bones were child's play. This would be easier than I initially thought.

Not only was this a test of my abilities to see how I stacked up against witches before we headed into a potential battle, but I owed him punishment for earlier. A lovely two-for-one scenario that made the cold-hearted bastard I was before Alina purr in my chest.

While she'd undoubtedly brought out a warmer version of me, this side of me would always be waiting within, itching for someone to cross those I loved.

"You fucking psycho!" he cried, turning his eyes toward Oleander, who sat unmoving in the chair with his back to us mere feet away. "Ollie! How are you going to let him do this to me here? I'm your family!"

It was a good question, and I was glad to know I was testing his loyalty already.

Oleander didn't bother turning to face Alexi before responding, venom dripping from every word. "You should be thankful he's handling your punishment, Alexi, because I promise you it is a lighter one than what I had intended for you."

Alexi balked, his face paling and bringing a sinister grin to my face as Oleander continued, "If that is how you're going to represent our family, by ruining relations with valued customers and prominent guests just for your own little thrill, you have no place in this business."

"I...I was just messing around!" the little vermin spluttered, his eyes bugging out as he pleaded with the back of Oleander's head. "Ollie, I'm sorry!"

Seeing as he hadn't used his shadows against me yet boded well. Did all Shadow witches need to use their hands to use their magic? Nimia had to touch her victim, and Alexi had to snap his fingers to use his.

I needed to be sure he wasn't holding them at bay just to appease Oleander. A wicked grin crossed my face. It was time to strike some real fear into his heart.

Pushing his face against the floor, I forced him closer to the fire, inch by delicious inch.

"What the fuck are you doing, you fucking psychopath?!" He tried to buck me off him, but I was much too strong for him to make even a half-decent attempt. His feet tried fervently to gain the traction needed to give him more force, but to no avail.

Heat licked deliciously against my hand as I held his face just outside the stone that lined the hearth. Leaning down until I was next to his ear, I growled, "Do not talk about my wife ever again. Do you understand me?"

Emphasizing my threat, I tilted his head forward until the burning scent of hair began to fill the air alongside his screams. What a delicious, heady mixture.

A sob ripped from his throat as he croaked, "I'm sorry. I'm so sorry. Please let me go!"

At this point, I was certain he would have used his powers if he could. Still, I didn't let up, wanting to push it just a bit further.

Excuse me, did I just hear you say wife? Did we get married while I was unconscious or something?

Alina's shock was adorable. Truly, she should have known better.

You're my mate, and maybe that's enough of a claim for the others, but I'm going to claim you with every fucking tradition that I can, Comoroă. I will be putting a ring on your finger as soon as we have a moment to breathe.

She didn't have a chance to respond before all of

our attention was pulled back to the spineless piece of shit still squirming beneath me. He thrashed and cried, sniffling loudly before whimpering in Oleander's direction.

"He's going to fucking kill me, and you're just sitting there with your new pet on your lap. Are you fucking kidding me, Ollie?"

Now that his pleas had fallen on deaf ears, he was resorting to insults. Wrong move.

Lo was no one's pet.

I snapped, and so did Oleander. In my peripheral line of vision, I saw him place Lo tenderly on the couch I had shared with Alina minutes before.

Switching my grip to Alexi's neck, I picked him up with a single hand, lifting him in the air until his feet dangled. I bared my teeth at him as he tried to claw at my hand, failing miserably with his broken fingers.

His face began to turn a beautiful shade of purple before I finally let him fall to the ground at Oleander's feet. He could deal with him from here— I'd gotten the answers I needed.

The glint of a blade flashed as Oleander dropped to a crouch above the coughing, shuddering Alexi. As the younger witch attempted to push himself up off the ground, the tip of Oleander's blade dug into the back of his neck.

"By all means, continue to try to get up, Alexi. I'd love to see the outcome," Oleander encouraged in a scarily calm voice that had even my hackles rising.

A manic glint flashed in his eyes, reflecting the flames of the raging fire in front of them. He was out for blood. And I was more than pleased by that fact.

While I hadn't intended for his dedication to Lo to be put to the test during my little trial, this act was exactly what I needed to see to back up his earlier words. He wouldn't allow his family to disrespect her in the slightest. As if by magic, all of my earlier concerns vanished into thin air.

Alexi gave up his struggle as the blade kissed his skin, and a rivulet of blood trickled down his neck. He flattened to the floor as he muttered, "I'm sorry. I was just fucking scared and said whatever came to mind."

A tsking sound came from Oleander as he twirled the hilt of the knife around in his hand, using Alexi's neck as a platform, no doubt cutting deeper into his skin with the move. "You should have thought twice before talking about *my mate* that way, Alexi. Luckily for you, I'm feeling gracious. I'll give you some extra time to think about your actions. Come up with a worthy apology because you'll be groveling at her feet for forgiveness the moment she wakes up."

His words pulled a satisfied chuckle from me.

Oleander's finger swirled in the air, and as his shadows appeared, they consumed Alexi's body. The younger man vanished from our sight within seconds.

As if that entire situation hadn't actually transpired, Oleander tucked his knife away before calmly padding over to gather Lo in his arms again.

Holy hell. I definitely trust him with her now.

Crossing to my own mate, I tucked her against my side, dropping a kiss on the top of her head.

Same here, Comoroă. We can focus fully on our mission with the knowledge that she is safe here.

Oleander started walking down a different hallway that led further into the house, taking Lo with him. Calling out over his shoulder, he yelled, "Come this way, and I'll get you everything you need, as well as answer any last-minute questions you may have."

Lincoln and I shared a look before he muttered, "He's a little unhinged, don't you think? I mean, with the way he snapped from violence to being a calm host in a matter of seconds."

His observation pulled a chuckle from Alina as she glanced between us. Her smile was wide as she rebutted, "Oh, and the three of us and Andrei aren't a little unhinged? He fits in great, if you ask me."

I couldn't help the laugh that spilled from my lips at her offhand comment. I guess we were a bunch of possessive and territorial psychopaths when it came to the people we loved.

I wouldn't have it any other way.

CHAPTER FIVE
ALINA

Under the cover of night, we set out with the map provided by Oleander. Now that we could use our speed and had replenished some of our energy with the bags of blood Oleander had given us, it should be a quick journey into the mountain.

A tinge of exhaustion had my body feeling sluggish as I pumped my arms at my sides, willing myself to run faster. Despite having the sustenance to curb my hunger, I knew the unsettled feeling swirling inside of me was due to the lack of sleep. I had to shake it off and focus—I'd crash into a bed and hibernate as soon as we got Lo home.

My eyes darted around the rocky terrain as we ascended the mountain, scouring the area for enemies. Despite the ease I felt with Lo being as safe as she could be, the edge of the unknown ran beneath my skin like a live wire. All of my senses felt overloaded, like they were on high alert.

We continued to run in silence, with Drake leading the way and Lincoln at my back, until we saw the faint orange glow of lights in the distance. *Bingo.* From this far away, they were just small dots, but seeing them gave me a sense of relief. We were getting closer to finding the antidote. My eyes zeroed in on our target.

I didn't care what we had to do to get it—we would not leave empty-handed.

The higher we got in altitude on the mountain range, the more my chest burned from the thin air. I refused to ask for a break as the large, dark silhouette of the hideout became more visible against the ghostly night sky. If Lincoln and Drake could make it, so could I. I refused to be the one holding us back when Lo's life hung in the balance.

We couldn't be Lo and Al without Lo.

Sweat dampened my brow, and I wiped it continuously to keep it from falling into my eyes. Barreling through the darkness up the final incline toward our target, we slowed our speed before coming to a complete stop behind a natural rocky corner that provided cover. Bending at the waist and resting my palms on my knees, I took deep, ragged breaths.

Giving Lincoln and Drake a once-over, a growl of annoyance bubbled in my chest at the sight of them standing there, seemingly unfazed by our marathon sprint. Show-offs.

While I knew they were stronger and older than me, it still chapped my ass to think of myself as inferior to them. I wanted to be their equal, ensuring they knew I wasn't a liability and that they could depend on me. My training had fallen by the wayside recently, and I was feeling it with my exhaustion.

We were still far enough away that it felt safe to speak, so I risked whispering for everyone's sake instead of depending on multiple one-on-one mental conversations. "How should we play this?" I panted. "Do we walk up, calm, cool, and collected, and state that we want a meeting with Arachne? Or do we go in kicking ass and taking names?"

When Oleander initially told us Astaroth's second-in-command's name, I honestly laughed. Arachne. It was so fitting for a bad guy.

My heart beat faster and faster in my chest, and the knowledge of how high the stakes were was putting me on edge. We couldn't afford to make the wrong decision here.

"We stand and observe before deciding," Lincoln instantly answered, shifting to get a better view.

I took the moment of reprieve to breathe deeply and take in the fortress before us.

Its high levels, strewn with countless windows, stared back at me like dark, lifeless eyes gazing into the night. The dark brick walls allowed the structure to blend into the mountain from a distance, but up close, it looked like a prison. The first floor gave us a glimpse of the inside, dimly lit by the warm-toned lights we'd seen from the distance. On the roof's peak, a chimney wafted plumes of smoke into the sky.

The childish part of me wondered if there was a boiling cauldron next to the chimney they roasted children in for stew.

In all regards, it was a normal-looking home and not what I was expecting from an evil witch's lair. What perfectly matched the vibe I was expecting was the noise—or the lack of it.

It was eerily silent, as if something evil had taken hold of it, and no one dared to disturb it, animal or human. For a massive structure that was supposed to be a hideout for witches who followed

Astaroth, shouldn't there have been movement inside or guards outside chatting? You know, the typical hustle and bustle of a base.

What was it with the witches here? Did no one ever fear for their safety?

Typically, I would have just blown into their fortress, kicking ass until I found the person I needed and threatening them until I got what I wanted. But this time, there were too many unknown variables in this situation for my usual course of action. Anxiety clawed at my stomach. I missed the confident steel that normally held my back straight and my head high as I went into any situation. I had a feeling I was going to need to find it—and quickly.

"I'm going to move forward alone to try to scout out the interior," Lincoln stated, but I grabbed his arm before he could bolt off, yanking him back.

Giving him a look of fury, I whisper-yelled, "Absolutely not! We are not splitting up here. We move together as one."

His mouth opened, looking like he was getting ready to argue, but after I held his gaze for a few tense beats, he snapped it shut. I don't know what he saw on my face that made him not argue with me for control, but I was thankful nonetheless. This wasn't the time or the place for us to have our typical power struggle.

There was just something about magic that had me in a constant state of unease, and I wanted my men to stay close to me. The hair on the back of my neck stood on end, and despite us not seeing anyone, deep down, I knew we were being watched like prey.

I wanted us to get the fuck out of Carmina as quickly as we could. I could always count on my skills against vampires in hand-to-hand combat, but this was well outside what I felt confident with. It also wasn't just me that I had to worry about anymore. If Lincoln or Drake were hurt or taken from me... My chest squeezed at the thought. I couldn't even imagine the lengths I would go to get them back. I'd steal their souls back from the after-life if that's what it took.

Drake let out a grunt from my left. "I have to say, I agree with our girl. Let's stay together and head to the door. At this rate, I'm beginning to think they knew of our presence in Carmina well before we began our trek here tonight. This perimeter is nothing like Oleander warned us of. They've made too many changes to their security."

According to Oleander's intel, there was

supposed to be a patrol of Blood and Shadow witches at all times. He said we'd be able to tell who was a Shadow witch based on their lack of physical weapons while they were on guard. Apparently, Shadow witches could conjure weapons with their powers, while Blood witches relied on the tried-and-true physical ones we all used.

Blood witches weren't as adept at using their powers for offensive attacks. Their energy was mostly used for potions and small spells, but they could heal their wounds almost instantly, which made them formidable in a different way.

I'd feared how we were going to combat a squadron of them, but it appeared as if there was an entirely different reason to be afraid. They knew we were coming, despite our best efforts to stay concealed.

"I agree," I piped up, my throat feeling thick with nerves as I swallowed hard.

"Alright then," Lincoln agreed with a heavy huff, his head shaking slightly as his eyebrows rose in concern. "Let's go into the lair of snakes. Stay alert, and don't make any rash moves."

His eyes and words were pointed toward me, so I narrowed my eyes back at him before turning toward the front of the building.

How dare he act like I was the only one we had to worry about? I was not the only loose cannon in this group. Our little rhombus was practically a ticking time bomb.

I love you, Princess, reckless behavior and all.

I still wasn't used to hearing those three little words from any of my mates, and it caught me off guard. His words of affection warmed my heart, bringing a small smile to my face as I blew him a quick kiss.

I love you too, Sir, pain in the ass behavior and all.

His hand brushed over my back as he fell in step at my side, reminding me that I wasn't alone in this and filling me with a small dose of confidence that I desperately needed.

As we approached, the gravel churned beneath our boots on the path. I was flanked on either side, and while I trusted Lincoln and Drake, I desperately wanted Andrei here with us. We were more powerful as a unit, and I'd seen his display of prowess at school as well as the night the castle had been raided. Not only would having him here give us a bigger tactical edge, but I selfishly missed him, too, despite not being apart for long. As cliché as it sounded, it *did* feel like there was a hole in my heart left from being apart from him, and I knew I wouldn't feel whole until I was back with him.

We'll be reunited soon, Comoroă. And if you promise to be a good girl and not do anything reckless with the witches, I promise to let Andrei partake in our shower next time.

A surge of emotions rushed within me, both annoyance and desire filling me as I glanced at him. He kept his gaze on the looming structure before us, not a single emotion on his face indicating that he had just offered to rail me with two other vampires simultaneously. Nope, you'd think he was just on an average weekday stroll.

I faced forward again and scowled as we stepped onto the doorstep. Why did they keep acting like I was such a flight risk?

You really have *no* idea why, Alina? Not even the slightest?

You do pop up at the best times, Dev. You should put those skills on your resume.

Ha, ha. Very funny. But answer me this, brat —would you give up your life for them?

My answer was swift and easy. *Yes.*

They know that, you fucking idiot. That's why they keep acting like that. They're nervous that you'll do something reckless—for them.

Before I could answer, the large wooden doors swung open unprompted. The motion stole my focus as the light from inside poured over us and backlit a witch who looked way too smug.

So *this* was Arachne, Astaroth's second-in-command at this location. His identity was easy enough to deduce just by the arrogant energy radiating off him as he took us in one by one.

The man's face was chiseled and smooth, with a strong jawline and high cheekbones. His hair was a dark chocolate brown, short and well-kept, and his eyes were a luminous shade of silver. His body was slim and athletic, with broad shoulders and long legs that were clad in black dress pants. He wore a matching dress shirt with the sleeves rolled up to the elbows, showing off tanned skin that was covered by black spiderweb tattoos that extended from the top of his hand all the way to his elbow.

My brows raised at the markings—how fitting for his name. I wonder which came first—the name or his tattoos.

He flashed us a smile full of pearly-white, straight teeth before taking a sip of the amber liquid swirling in his glass. Smacking his lips together after he swallowed, I couldn't help the way my features screwed up in annoyance as he murmured,

"This scotch was aged perfectly. I'd pour you all a glass, but you took so long getting here that I drank it all."

If my mouth didn't say how much he annoyed me, my face sure would, even though I was trying my best to look civil.

"I've been awaiting your arrival since one of my acquaintances spotted you in our central city. What took you so long?" he questioned, pulling the door open further and leaning against the large door frame like we were family with a standing invitation.

Don't answer—let's see what he spews out.

When none of us responded, his smile fell, and he offered us a look of dejection as he held his free hand over his heart. "Oh, come now, don't tell me there's someone else here that you wanted to see first! I'm hurt that I wasn't your priority."

Oleander warned us he would offer a charming facade, lying with every other breath to manipulate people into getting what he wanted, so I would be remiss to give into this little chat, even without Drake's command to not answer.

Honestly, at this point, I was curious about how long he would continue to have a one-sided conversation. If we weren't in such a precarious position,

I'd really milk it for all I could for a good laugh at his expense.

He tipped his glass up to his lips once more, sucking a piece of ice into his mouth before crunching on it loudly. With an annoying smirk on his face as he looked us over, he nodded to himself. "Don't fret about the late arrival, though, friends. It gave me a chance to talk about this little situation with the bossman. You know, Astaroth."

At the mention of the piece of shit responsible for so much heartbreak in my life, a growl slipped from my lips. I took a fraction of a step forward.

Spitfire—don't you dare.

Arachne raised a single brow at me, the charming ploy giving way to one of calculated thrill as he grinned again. "There she is, Alina Van Helsing —the last of her name. How's that feel, by the way?" he asked, furrowing his brows together as his smile vanished like he was deep in thought. "You can't change your name if you get married now—it would be such a pity if the name *died*..." He trailed off, looking at me pointedly, as if he were waiting for me to understand the punchline of a joke.

Unbridled fury radiated from within me, and I trembled with the force of it. The anger coursed through my veins like an overflowing river, a torrent of emotion ready to unleash destruction.

Let me kill him. We'll find another Blood witch.

My chest was on fire, burning with rage at the nonchalant way he talked about the slaughter of my goddamn family. My fists were clenched tightly at my sides, my nails digging into my palms and letting a trickle of blood flow.

I was so fucking close to giving into Dev's request, but Drake's voice broke through my violent thoughts.

Think of Lo.

I didn't hesitate with my request back to him. *Can I kill him once we get the antidote?*

I wouldn't let Arachne rile me enough to ruin the chance to get the cure, no matter how much my body vibrated with the blood haze coming over me. However, I sure as shit wanted to know if I could make him bleed after we got what we needed.

To be determined, little killer.

Arachne's hand snapped forward, grabbing my wrist. He practically purred as he looked at the blood trailing down my skin, his tongue darting out to wet his lips. "We can't let this delicacy go to waste, now can we? How about we make a deal, little slayer, and I'll take the blood now?"

Lincoln and Drake tensed at my side, but I quickly reassured them through our bond that I wouldn't give the witch my blood. That would be the absolute worst-case scenario.

Arachne's piercing silver eyes shifted from my hand to my face as I ripped my hand free from his hold and took a step back.

It was time to take control of this situation and not play the meek mouse. I was Alina Van Helsing, as he so kindly reminded me. I didn't cower for anyone.

"I haven't stated everything I want from you yet, Arachne," I said, tsking, letting condescension drip from every word. "You're so quick to offer a deal without knowing my terms. How fucking arrogant of you."

You better know what you're doing right now, Spitfire.

I didn't, but no one else needed to know that. I was trusting my gut.

CHAPTER SIX
ALINA

A deep laugh bellowed from Arachne as he backed up into the home, turning his back to us as he began walking away.

My mouth dropped open at the blatant dismissal and, even worse, the show of power. He wasn't concerned about giving us an opening to hurt him, and that type of confidence either came from extreme power or extreme stupidity. The latter wasn't likely, seeing as he was second-in command-here. Either way, it was fucking insulting, and I couldn't help the way my lips curled into a snarl.

No part of him feared us or what we could do, and it was becoming increasingly harder to keep my very large ego locked down. Never in my life had someone so blatantly scoffed in my face.

Drake stepped into the dimly lit home and called out to Arachne's retreating back, "Why would we make a deal with you when it's the three of us against you? We could just torture you until you gave it up."

Smart.

Instantly, I knew he was baiting Arachne into showing his hand by throwing the challenge out. We needed to know where the hell all the guards were. There wasn't a chance we had Arachne to ourselves. Better to know now, on our terms.

It was kind of scary how in tune I was becoming with my mates after such a short time together, but being connected to each other's minds really helped that process along.

"We both know that that's not true," Arachne answered with a dark chuckle, coming to a halt and turning on his heel to face us. His head tilted ever so slightly to the side. "Don't insult my intelligence, Dracula. But if you wish to see my forces, by all means."

With a flourish of his hand, the dimly lit foyer was suddenly lined with guards along the shadowed walls. A sharp kick to my back had me stumbling forward, barely catching myself before I face-planted into the tiled floor.

"What the fuck!" I seethed, whirling around in time to see a line of guards shoving a snarling Lincoln inside and to the ground with their shadows, restraining him as he snarled and looked around for me.

The doors slammed shut, trapping us.

As our eyes met, my stomach churned at the relief in his eyes when he saw me. It didn't seem like he cared that he was being engulfed by shadows, not when I seemed to be okay. I was frozen with fear as he began to quickly disappear, until only his eyes were visible.

Blood began to pour from the inside corners of his eyes.

No, *no*. This was not happening right now.

It doesn't matter what happens to me as long as you are safe.

His words horrified me, and I blinked furiously at him, seething at the notion.

No. That's not how this fucking works. You wouldn't let me sacrifice myself for you, so you aren't allowed to do the same. You better fucking hang on!

As I craned my head around, desperately searching for Drake, a gasp caught in my throat when I saw him snarling on his knees with a few dead witches around him. He was completely lost to his monster. I didn't understand why he was on his knees, though, his chest heaving and eyes trained behind me. If he was able to kill them, why would he just submit?

What the fuck was going on?

What was I going to do about it?

What *could* I do?

Dread crawled up my neck as I turned around completely, finding Arachne leaning against a dark corner of the room. He swirled the liquid in a small glass vial pinched between his fingers as he beamed a smile at me.

"This is what you came for, isn't it?" he goaded, lifting his hand high, the glass and liquid contents sparkling from the warm lights around us.

My eyes widened. The antidote.

He dropped it, and my stomach lurched in the second before he reached out with his other hand to snatch it out of the air, laughing maniacally to himself. A gasp of relief came from me as my hand flew to my chest, and he pulled the vial close and tucked it into the pocket of his dress shirt. Fucking bastard. He patted it gently before shoving his hands into his pant pockets and tilting his head at me, as if he were daring me to make a move now.

I had to do something. Lincoln was in dire trouble, and Drake was afraid to do anything with Arachne near me.

"What do you want in exchange for the antidote and our freedom?" I growled, spreading my feet in a ready-to-fight stance.

One corner of his lips tugged into a smirk as he pushed off the wall and strolled forward until he was chest-to-chest with me. "Well, you see..." he trailed off, lifting his fingers up to caress my jaw with the back of his knuckles and making a shiver of disgust roll through me as I stared at him, unflinching. "Astaroth would have been happy to make a deal for a vial of your blood for the antidote, but now that you've opened that mouth of yours, I'm curious to see what else it can do."

From behind me, I heard a loud roar from Drake, followed by grunts of pain.

My lips thinned. That's it—fuck this.

It was obvious that a polite and cordial meeting wasn't on the table anymore. If they wanted to show their force, so would I. I wasn't going to let anyone intimidate me or my mates, and I sure as hell wasn't going to let them hurt us. I'd been through too fucking much in this life to cower or kiss anyone's ass. Maybe if Arachne learned to fear me, he'd be more pliable and willing to give us what we needed.

I wasn't sure how many of these fuckers I could take out alone or if Dev's flames would work on the witches like they did vampires, but a good old-fashioned beheading would surely take a witch out.

We can take them. Believe in us, and our power will do the rest.

Reopening the wound on my palm, I held Arachne's gaze as I murmured, *"Devorare."*

The comforting feeling of her cool, steel hilt formed in my palm, and instantly, the confidence I yearned to feel in my spine flowed through me. Time felt as if it slowed as I gave up all control and opened mine and Dev's bond. We were one. There was no need for her to tell me what to do because her thoughts were one with my movements.

All sound faded away, and I shut off my mental connection to my mates as I focused solely on what I needed to do. Arachne registered my sword's appearance too late—I already had the butt of her hilt crashing into his temple. I didn't take time to gloat over his slumped body, instead turning back around and focusing on saving Lincoln from that mass of shadows that continued to swirl around him. No part of him was visible anymore.

Make them know our name—not for what has happened to the Van Helsings—but for what

we are capable of now when anyone dares cross us.

Goosebumps pebbled over my flesh at her words.

She was right. I was going to send a fucking message—right here and now—and I couldn't wait for it to reach Astaroth's ears. Because even if I couldn't face him today, one day I'd lend a hand to the Nyx family to aid in his destruction.

Pointing the tip of Devorare at the mass, and without stopping to second guess how I knew she could, I willed her to incinerate the shadows before they could kill him. A new kind of flame burst from my sword—a bright purple that appeared to be so high in heat that the center of it was a bluish-white.

My lips curled up into a smile that had to look sinister with the thirst for blood I knew was in my eyes as I watched the flames disintegrate the shadows around Lincoln. As soon as I saw him gasping on the floor, firmly alive, I turned my attention to the shadow witches who had done this to him. My purple flames crawled up their bodies, dragging them to the ground as screams poured from their mouths.

My brain signaled an alert from my peripheral line of vision, and I quickly swung Devorare around in a wide arc, sending out the same flame without looking, trusting my gut. By the time I saw the Blood witches with their swords pointed at me, the steel in their hands was melting into puddles on the ground before the flames laid into them, too. The force of the flames opened large gashes on their bodies as their clothes burned away, sending them to the floor just like the Shadow witches. Initially, I feared they would be able to heal the wounds with their powers, like Oleander had informed us, and continue to come at me, but they stayed down, writhing in agony.

"Let's go, motherfuckers," I whispered, taking a large inhale and preparing myself for more attacks as I glanced around us.

The twenty or so witches in the room with us were down for the count, and I expected more witches to pour in. But none appeared.

Drake flashed over to Lincoln, helping him to his feet so he could stumble toward me.

My nostrils flared at the putrid scent of burning skin and hair. An addictive feeling of power rolled through me, setting all the hair on my body on end as I turned back to Arachne's body.

Leaning over him, I grabbed the vial from his pocket and held it out to Drake. "Take this."

After he grunted and tucked it into his pocket, I turned and backhanded Arachne's cheek as I shouted, "Wake up, asshole!"

He grunted, slowly coming to, as his eyes opened, unfocused and disoriented. I loved watching the memories of what had happened right before he lost consciousness come rushing back to him. He stared at me in horror before glancing behind me for his backup, eyes wide with fear as his mouth opened in shock at the sight of all of his guards down.

I let my fangs lengthen as I cooed, "Now that right there is what I love to see, Arachne. The moment an arrogant piece of shit realizes he's not at the top of the food chain."

A girl could get used to this, whatever this new power was.

My name means *to devour*, Alina. You know that. But the thing is, I wasn't just built to devour vampires with my flames. I was made to devour *all* creatures and their magic.

Holy fucking shit. Her words from when we'd smited the board members who broke into the castle came rushing back to me.

"My power is beyond that of a normal soul weapon. I needed to be wielded by someone who wouldn't abuse the

power and think of themselves as judge, jury, and executioner."

The power was only meant to be used in dire circumstances, but it would have been nice to know ahead of time that it was an option.

You couldn't have told me this earlier when I was panicking about how we were going to face these witches?!

The power within me is for you to discover when you need it. You have to open your soul to it and trust in our power more and more to discover these facets of it. It's not something that can be taught in training. You have to unlock it.

Finally, Arachne's body caught up to the panic in his brain, and as he tried to scramble away on his hands and ass, Drake was quick to move behind him. I was relieved to see Lincoln standing on his own, drinking a bag of blood that seemed to have appeared out of thin air, but I couldn't help but wonder where the hell he'd gotten it from.

Drake brought blood from Oleander's stash to use on the off chance we had to provide a vial of blood and could slip it in.

And neither of you wanted to let me in on that little plan?

A wry smile slipped over his lips. *Nope.*

My head shook softly at that. Fuckers.

"Leaving so soon, friend?" I cooed at Arachne as Drake kicked him in the back, sending him sprawling onto his stomach as he clipped his chin against the floor near me.

I was having too much fun turning the tables on Arachne—I could do this all day—but I was truthfully only keeping him alive to ensure this was, in fact, the correct antidote.

I closed the few feet between us and pressed my boot onto his upper back. My sword, still streaming with purple flames, was held just outside the reach of his neck.

Instead of lashing out at me as I'd expected, he pleaded, "I'll give you whatever you want. Astaroth's location, the antidote, anything—name it. Just don't kill me."

Oleander had been correct. These witches had no loyalty. Instead, they were completely in it for themselves. It was the same as Jeoffrey and Rin. When would these people realize that they'd never succeed with that mindset? They'd never have a circle of people around them that would do anything to see them succeed because everyone was looking for the next best thing.

Deciding to stop playing with my food, I cut the

sarcastic and condescending quips from my mind that were waiting to flow out. My tone was cold and sharp as I barked, "I already have the antidote—from your shirt, you fucking moron."

His voice trembled as he attempted to look up at me from under his brows. "That's...that's not it. It's in my office—third door on the right, second floor, inside the drawer. Shimmering blue liquid. That one was a decoy."

I gave Drake a look, and he nodded before taking off.

I inched the blade closer, allowing the smallest edge of the flame to touch his skin, and it instantly burned the flesh there and made him scream.

"How do I know you're telling the truth, Blood Witch?"

Got it, Comoroă. Ask him if he'll drink a part of it to prove it.

"I have no reason to lie! I want to fucking live!" Arachne screamed, spit flying from his mouth, as I pulled the blade back.

I'd be putting that claim to the test.

"Drink a small amount to prove it's a cure. It shouldn't hurt you, right?"

A strangled sound came from him as his eyes bugged out at my demand. "It's meant to erase all traces of Blood magic from someone's system! I can't drink that—are you fucking crazy?"

How fucking perfect. Truly, I couldn't have planned this to be any more perfect than it was turning out to be.

A cold, detached laugh came from me. "You have absolutely no idea just how fucking crazy I am. Either drink the potion and lose your powers, or you'll be known as Arachne, last of his fucking name, on your tombstone."

His throat bobbed heavily as he stared at me with wide, fearful eyes. I sure as shit bet he was regretting the way he'd goaded me over my family's deaths now that his life was in my hands.

There was nothing quite like the rush of adrenaline one got while exacting vengeance. It tasted so delicious.

The crazy part was that I didn't come here with the intention of killing him. My beef was with Astaroth, and if Arachne would have just accepted our appearance and treated it like a business transaction, we would have been on our way. He brought this entirely upon himself, and not a single ounce of my cold, black heart would feel bad watching the light leave his eyes if this killed him.

Although... I had to admit that the option of him

living without his powers for the rest of his life was an even more enticing offer. Dissolved to the status of a mere mortal—that would be agony for someone who thought so damn highly of himself.

When Drake returned, we exchanged a nod before he crouched down by the witch's head, opening the vial and putting it against his tightly closed lips.

"Choose now, Arachne," I demanded, bringing Dev's blade closer once more. "Or we choose for you."

He let out a growl. "Fine! Fucking fine!" he exclaimed before opening his mouth.

It went without saying that we weren't going to waste much of the antidote. Drake proceeded to let three small drops fall into Arachne's mouth before using his free hand to shove his jaw closed to keep him from spitting the liquid out.

"Swallow," Drake commanded, staring down at the pathetic witch.

I cleared my throat, uncomfortably enjoying the command and power of his tone.

You wouldn't make me command that of you, would you, Comoroă? You're a good girl, and you want to swallow for me.

Fucking hell.

The brief, sexually charged moment was shattered by Arachne's body convulsing. His eyes rolled back in his head until only the whites were visible. His mouth sagged open in a contorted, quiet scream.

We took a few steps back until all three of us stood in a line at his side, waiting for his reaction to end and to make sure he was actually alive. The wait felt like an eternity, but I knew it was probably just because of the ticking clock we had on our heads with Lo.

Eventually, he came to a rest, flat on his back, his eyes staring up at the ceiling, void of fight or emotion. Empty.

Just how I wanted him.

Now maybe he'd feel the smallest sliver of the void I felt, losing the thing I loved most in this world. For me, it was when my family was brutally ripped away from me, but for him, I knew it would be having his power ripped from him.

"Happy now?" he asked, his tone cold and flat.

Now that he was powerless, it was my turn to give him my back, and damn, it felt good.

"Yes, yes I am," I practically sang as we walked out the door, antidote in hand.

It was time to save my best friend.

CHAPTER SEVEN
LINCOLN

Lo's screams could be heard through the walls of the manor as we approached. The sound was piercing not only our eardrums but also our hearts, if the looks on Alina and Drake's faces were an indicator.

Their eyes squeezed shut for a brief moment as their faces contorted into a mask of agony, as if they were in a battle with their own souls, trying to block out the sounds of suffering that surrounded us. Their hands grasped one another tightly, a sign of solidarity against the harsh reality we faced.

Tears streamed down Alina's cheeks, barely visible in the night, before they were swept away by the wind in our sprint. Their combined agony poured off of them in waves, and they were unable to keep a barrier up in their distressed states.

It fucking tore me up inside to watch Alina in pain like this, knowing there was nothing I could do besides continue to run at their sides until we got the antidote to Lo. As much as I had issues with Drake from my childhood, I had to admit that he was growing on me, and it brought me no joy to feel his pain. I was beginning to think that maybe the childish lens through which I'd viewed those events might not have been the reality of them. Perhaps in my emotional and distraught state, he'd not played as heavy a hand in the way I'd been dismissed after my parents' deaths as I thought. In all regards, he has been proving himself to me day after day since coming into our lives.

I sent them both the same thought, imbuing my words with as much confidence as I could muster.

She's still alive—as much as we hate hearing her screams, it means she's alive. Do not give up hope.

They didn't need to respond, but I felt the way their minds grasped onto my words like lifelines, and it brought instant relief to the tightness in my chest that they were both receptive to what I said.

Closing in on the house, we didn't slow down. We didn't bother with the formalities of knocking, either. Instead, I broke the lock open with a swift kick to the door and ran straight into the room where we'd left them.

Lo writhed in agony, her skin paler than I'd ever seen and damp with sweat. Her face was contorted in pain, and her eyes were tightly shut. Oleander's face twisted with worry as he held her in his arms, his hands trembling as he attempted to comfort her with gentle motions and soft words.

"Angel," he murmured, pressing his lips to her forehead as his eyes shut. "Please fight. Fight for you. Fight for me. Fight for *us*."

Emotion clogged my throat at the sight, my windpipe suddenly feeling like it'd shrunk ten sizes. Fuck. They'd just found each other. It couldn't end here. If Alina and I had never had the opportunity to explore our bond... My hands shook at my sides at the mere thought.

It was unthinkable.

As he opened his eyes and looked at us, tears pooled in their depths before a single one rolled down his cheek. "Please tell me you have the antidote. She doesn't have much longer."

Drake rushed forward, falling to his knees as he scrambled for the vial in his pocket. He fumbled with the lid, and I turned my focus on Alina, taking in her shaking body as she watched in horror, barely looking like she was breathing herself.

She pulled her hand up to cover her mouth as she watched, and I couldn't help but drag her against my side, holding her as tightly as Oleander held Lo. Instantly, at my touch, she buried her head in my chest, like she couldn't bear to watch.

I can't, Linc. I can't watch another friend die.

My heart shattered for the incredible woman in my arms, the one who'd had to endure far too much in her life.

I sent as much conviction and strength back to her with my words. *She's not going to die, Alina. She's not.*

While Lo's survival wasn't something I could promise or swear, it was what I willed the universe to make come true. *You've let me down so many fucking times—give me this for my mate. You owe her this.*

Fuck, it owed her so much for what she'd suffered through.

I held the back of her head as her tears soaked through my shirt and her fist balled against my abdomen.

Oleander held Lo's mouth open as Drake lifted the vial to her lips. They let the antidote pour into her mouth before they worked her neck and head into an angle where it could run down her throat.

Nerves ate away at my stomach as we waited with bated breath to see if it would work. The only sound filling the room was the crackling of the wood in the fireplaces as Lo's screams slowly died away. My eyes tracked the hands of the grandfather clock in the corner as they moved slowly, ticking away the seconds of an eternity.

Tension climbed with each passing second, and the room felt charged with electricity.

Out of nowhere, Lo sucked in a huge lungful of air as she bolted up, colliding with Oleander's forehead, which had hovered above her.

"What the fuck!" she yelled, pulling back as her brows furrowed in pain, rubbing at the skin already turning red from the collision.

She was back. Holy shit. We did it.

Relief crashed through me like a tidal wave. While Lo and I didn't have the same relationship as Drake and Alina did with her, she was still a part of our family. From our limited time together and what I knew of her through them, she was an incredible soul.

If she hadn't made it, it would absolutely be a colder world without her in it.

Alina scrambled from my arms, jumping over Drake, who stared at Lo with a goofy fucking grin and a few tears running down his face.

"Lo!" she yelled, grabbing her from Oleander's arms and falling onto the floor with her in a pile of tangled limbs.

"Alina, what's going on?" Lo asked breathlessly, seemingly in a daze, as she attempted to push herself off the ground. I wasn't sure if it was from the Blood magic, headbutting Oleander, or Alina tackling her to the ground.

Poor thing.

Oleander let out a feral growl, and instantly I was on edge. I bolted to step between him and the women, but Drake beat me to it, holding a black-claw-tipped hand to the witch's chest as he rumbled, "Back off, Oleander. Alina would never hurt her. She's just excited."

I knew it didn't matter to Oleander at that moment, though. He was blinded by his overwhelming desire to protect and nurture Lo—and likely to claim her as well now that she was awake. While I was sympathetic to this unusual and emotionally traumatic beginning to a mate bond, I wasn't going to let him treat Alina like a villain. Not after what we went through to get Lo back.

Alina ignored all of us, focusing entirely on Lo as they both sat up, checking her over like a fussy mother hen. Lo quickly stopped her, though, grabbing Alina's hands and muttering, "Stop. I'm fine, Al. It's all coming back to me now, but where—"

As Lo's eyes traveled around the room, I saw the moment her entire world came to a screeching halt, everything failing to exist except her and Oleander. He stopped struggling against Drake, suddenly looking as tame as a kitten, his mouth parting and his eyes widening in wonder as he held her gaze for the first time.

Alina rose, moving to Drake and dragging him from between Lo and Oleander and over to me, giving them their moment to do with it as they wished. So much adoration poured from Alina through our bond as we watched Oleander slowly walk toward Lo and offer her his hand.

A blush stained Lo's cheeks as she placed her hand in his, allowing him to pull her to her feet before pressing his lips to the top of her hand.

"It's a pleasure to finally meet you, Angel," he murmured as he glanced at her over the top of her hand.

As he straightened to his full height, it forced Lo to crane her head up to maintain eye contact with him. Neither of them let go of the other's hand as she attempted to ask, "Are you... Are we..." She trailed off and looked at us with wide, searching eyes, as if we had the answers she already held within her soul.

That was the thing about mate bonds—they were different for each individual. Although Alina and I had an undeniable pull to each other, neither of us had known what that electric energy was. If you asked Drake, he knew from the moment he laid eyes on Alina that she was his.

The only people who could confirm the bond were them, and it felt like an incredibly intimate moment to be witnessing all of a sudden.

Should we...go?

Drake's eyes swung toward me at the question, and his indecision was projected very fucking loudly without words.

The goofy grin that had been on the face of the vampire everyone in Sanguis feared fell away, leaving him with a look of dejection and...acceptance. From the way his eyes fell from Lo to the floor and his entire body seemed to deflate, I suddenly felt like a dick with my suggestion, and I rushed to explain why.

I know we just got her back, but it feels like this is a

private moment they need to explore without us gawking at them.

He let out a heavy sigh as Alina leaned her head against my chest, completely enthralled as she watched the scene play out like a romance novel right before our eyes. There was no doubt within me that these two would have watched Oleander and Lo unashamedly for as long as they could.

"Oleander, Lo," Drake started, bursting their bubble of a moment and startling them as they seemed to remember we were here. "We're going to head back to the castle. We desperately need sleep and more blood. Do you...do you want to stay here for a while, Lo?"

I could feel the pain in his tone at the question, but I was really proud of him for putting her needs first and leaving the decision to her.

Lo's brow furrowed as she tugged her bottom lip between her teeth, chewing on both it and the question, it seemed.

Oleander stepped closer, gently prying her lip out from between her teeth as he whispered, "Do not feel like you have to stay here for me. We have all the time in the world to get to know each other, beautiful. You're welcome to stay as long as you'd like, but I'd understand if you wanted to go home with your family for now. You've been through a lot."

It didn't escape me the way he said *for now*, but nonetheless, it was big of him to not make her feel pressured into staying, given the way we'd seen him struggle to let her out of his hold while she was unconscious.

"I..." Lo stammered, looking between him and us like this was a defining moment, and while I couldn't give her any words of advice, I did give her a soft smile that I hoped came across as encouragement.

We'd support whatever decision she made.

Alina was quick to step in, coming to the same conclusion as me as I watched the indecision that plagued Lo.

"For what it's worth, Lo, he has our seal of approval," she offered softly, smiling earnestly at her friend. "He protected and cared for you when you were unconscious. Oleander was a complete gentleman—with a slightly unhinged possessiveness over you. But in the best way, just like my mates."

The comparison brought a chorus of chuckles through the room, doing an incredible job of lightening the serious tone that had developed amongst our group.

"I'm going to stay here for a bit," she finally answered with a single nod to herself, the pink stain once again coloring her cheeks as she glanced back at Oleander with a soft smile.

He nodded, seemingly pleased with her choice, before looking at us and offering, "I have a portal here for our witches to use for client services. You are welcome to use it to get home. You're also welcome to use it as a landing point if you ever need to visit."

My body practically sagged in relief at the realization that we didn't have to head back to town to use the portal in central Carmina. We all needed a shower and to collapse. We'd gone well past our reserves, using only our adrenaline to keep us running this long.

While there was still a hell of a lot to tackle with the news of the slayer family who betrayed Alina's, I desperately hoped she could find it within her to let herself rest and recharge for longer than a day. Not just for her sake but for all of ours as well.

After saying our goodbyes, we were escorted to the portal. Alina grabbed our hands, all of us pausing to look over our shoulders one last time.

Our new lovebirds had their foreheads pressed

together in an intimate gesture that spoke of respect, affection, and unity. Their eyes were closed as they took a moment to connect on a level so deep no one would ever understand until they experienced it for themselves.

She's going to be just fine.

Alina's eyes snagged mine as we turned back to the portal.

She's going to be more than all right if it ends up being even a fraction of the greatness I've experienced with you three.

Fuck, I loved this woman.

***

The second we stepped through the portal into the familiar walls of the castle, Alina squealed and took off at a full run before jumping straight into the arms of Andrei. He'd stood there with his arms open, as if he'd spent every second waiting near the door for her return.

Honestly, I wouldn't put it past him for that to be the truth.

Holding her in his arms, they shared a passionate kiss as I took note of the colorful bracelets hanging around his wrist. My eyes narrowed.

Those better not be what I think they are.

Drake announced he was going to do a sweep of the place after clapping Andrei on the back in greeting. Apparently, he needed to ensure his specifications were met with the team he'd hired to do repairs from the break-in to fortify the windows and doors.

The man never stopped. Just constantly go, go, go. But as he turned the corner, I saw the smile he'd forced in front of Andrei and Alina slip from his face, revealing an exhausted and anxious look in its place.

I wasn't sure if he wanted my support or if we'd even reached a level where me offering it was acceptable, but something felt like it had shifted since we took on both the board members and the situation in Carmina together.

Fuck it. I'd at least try. If he was a dick about it, I'd go back to our previously terse relationship—no skin off my back. But if we could learn to coexist in peace, I knew it would make Alina happy and all of our lives easier, so it was worth a shot.

Vic and Estrid would have beamed if they could see me now. The young vampire who came to DIA with a chip on his shoulder, vowing to never return to vampire society in Sanguis, now lending his support to the very vampire that he'd held so much resentment for once upon a time.

Giving Alina and Andrei a moment together, I sped after him, grabbing his shoulder to halt him. I didn't want to risk Alina hearing in case whatever was bothering him was something he wanted to keep private.

Are you okay?

He didn't turn around, but his head dropped forward, like he'd rather stare at his shoes than look into my face. All the tension bled from his body as his shoulders slumped forward.

His tone was solemn as he answered, ***I'm tired, brother.***

In my shock at the term of endearment, my hand fell to the side. Standing there, mouth slightly open, I stared at his back as he stepped away from me and continued his walk down the hall, eventually disappearing around the corner.

What the hell was that?

It only further served the thought that we all really needed a fucking moment to breathe and collect ourselves. It occurred to me then that we might have to have that conversation without Alina around to touch base. It was so hard-wired into her brain to never take a moment to breathe that I couldn't see her allowing herself more than a day before she was onto her next mission in her quest for vengeance.

Before I could process Drake's reaction any further, Alina called out for me, and I padded back until I spotted her smiling face standing next to Andrei. Quickly wiping off my concern and confusion, I returned the look before sweeping her into my arms and tilting her back as I pressed a trail of kisses up her neck until I found her lips.

Biting her bottom one lightly before flicking my tongue over it, I devoured the moment. For this one second in time, all that mattered was that we were all safe and I could hold my mate in my arms. Despite being together almost nonstop recently, I fucking missed her. I knew it sounded ridiculous, but I desperately needed time with her without the pressing weight of our fucked-up rhombus' cumulative problems that piled shit nonstop on our shoulders.

Andrei cleared his throat as I stood Alina back up with a final kiss.

"I have a present for you, Linc," he chirped, clearly back to his annoying self now that his dad was dead and his mother was safe.

Fucking hell. The things I put up with for Alina.

Before I even saw what was in his hand, I was

rolling my eyes. I knew what it was going to be. I fucking knew it, and I hated it. I didn't think he was actually going to follow through with it, but here we were.

Sure enough, in his outstretched hand was a fucking bracelet with a variety of letter beads in various colors.

I stared blankly at him as he shoved it toward me, a shit-eating grin on his face as he looked at Alina, who looked like she was attempting—and failing—to keep her shit together. "She already has hers on. Come on, take it."

Reaching out to grab it between my thumb and index finger, I let the bracelet dangle in the air like a diseased animal as I inspected it. My eyes scanned the letters, and a growl slipped from my lips.

"Andrei's BFF" was spelled out across the multi-colored beads in bold, white letters.

Sighing, I realized the best path was the one of least resistance, so I slid it onto my wrist. Hopefully, if I went along with it, Andrei wouldn't find it as funny, and I could toss it in the trash in a few days.

But as I let my wrist fall back to my side, he clapped me on the shoulder, a genuine smile on his face as he said, "I'm glad you all made it back safe, man." The tiniest sliver of my heart actually felt bad at the thought of him possibly finding the bracelet in the trash one day.

Damn it. I was growing too damn soft around them.

CHAPTER EIGHT
ALINA

After leaving Lincoln in the kitchen to make a few phone calls to DIA to check in—with a stern order from me to ask about Alexandra—I allowed Andrei to pull me upstairs with the promise of taking care of me.

My abdomen fluttered with the possibilities of what that meant. While I was spent physically and emotionally after the past forty-eight hours of hell, the idea of an orgasm felt like saving room for dessert after a full dinner. Just like a decadent dessert, I'd never turn down an orgasm.

It had been so incredibly hard to part ways with Andrei before going to Carmina, and it was strange to feel almost nervous and shy now that we were alone with all of that mess behind us. I was, and always would be, proud of my sexuality and my body, but we hadn't had a moment alone to explore one another since our mating, when we exchanged blood. Now that the moment was here... I felt like I didn't know what to do.

As he toyed with the dials of the shower, I stood behind him, twisting my fingers in front of me anxiously and watching the defined muscles of his tanned back stretch and flex with his movements.

My tongue darted out to wet my lips. So far, he'd only removed his shirt, but I was already getting so fucking worked up. If there was one thing I could thank the Fates for, it was how perfect my mates were.

The memory of him watching from outside this exact shower as Lincoln and Drake shared me had my thighs rubbing together and my cheeks flushing. Hopefully, he'd assume it was from the heat beginning to build in here.

When he turned around, there was a hunger in his eyes that had my clit pulsing, but my mouth popped open as my eyes focused on the black ink over three of his fingers that dangled at his side. I had to blink twice as I stared at it, feeling like I was imagining what I was seeing. Was that...a tattoo? How had I missed it earlier?

He prowled toward me, a knowing smirk on his face, as he backed me up against the bathroom wall until his presence engulfed me. Leaning over me, he rested his hand on the wall and murmured, "I was wondering when you were going to notice that, baby girl."

The intensity of his gaze and the heat emanating from his body almost convinced my brain to let go of the new tattoo and just jump him here and now, but I shook my head and forced myself to focus.

Down, girl, I mentally chastised my libido.

Grabbing his hand, I pulled it closer to my face for further inspection as he chuckled at me.

"Shut the fuck up," I breathed out as the truth of what was tattooed on his skin hit me.

A.V.H. was inked just above the middle knuckles on his pointer, middle, and ring fingers, respectively. My initials. Me—Alina Van Helsing, on Andrei Deluca's fingers.

Was this actually my life? In the twenty-four hours we'd been separated, he'd found the time to permanently have me etched onto his body.

For a moment, I was overwhelmed by what felt like all of our moments rushing back to my brain like a mini movie as I ran my finger gently over the letters and turned my gaze up to his, getting lost in his gorgeous green eyes and long, dark lashes as I reminisced.

The way I ran into his chest and felt his eyes on me even as the rest of the students clamored around him, wanting his attention. But his attention had always been mine.

When I sat between his legs at the party and we stared at the stars together. How he really showed me the tender side of him that lay beneath his cocky exterior.

The heartbreaking moment when we both thought we couldn't explore what was happening between us as we sat on the floor outside the training room.

When I found him outside my door, pouring his heart out to me and fighting for us because he knew in his soul we were meant to be, despite the odds.

Everything we went through with his father.

We'd overcome so fucking much, and now we were here. I was at a loss for words, completely lost in the desire pulsing through me and the love I had for him.

As I gazed up at Andrei with adoration for him bursting from within my chest, his hand came up to grab my chin tightly as he leaned in closer until his breath fanned across my lips. His musky, subtle scent of patchouli and sandalwood wrapped around us, invading my senses and making me mentally moan.

There was just something about a man that smelled good that made my knees weak.

"I told you back when we claimed each other that I wanted you to mark me—that I wanted the world to see that I'm yours, baby girl," he murmured, a smirk tugging the corner of his lips up. "I just took it upon myself to make the statement a little more permanent with the help of an acquaintance."

Fuck me, I was going to dissolve into a puddle and be swept down the shower drain alongside the boiling stream of water if I had to get in there in this state.

I answered in the only way I could—from the depths of my soul, as my heart sang in response to his sweet words. "I love you, Andrei Deluca. Forever."

His voice dropped into a low grumble as he asked, "But what if I want more than forever, baby girl? Would you give it to me?"

I blinked rapidly, searching for the words to respond to such a heart-melting question.

It came to me then as I pressed up onto my toes

to tease his lips with mine and stared deep into his eyes. "I can't give you something you already have."

A rumble rolled through his chest, vibrating through mine as he pressed in closely, erasing all distance between us.

"Good answer, baby girl," he praised.

Holding his stare, I whispered, "Does that mean you don't need me to mark you anymore since you've done it permanently?"

His green eyes narrowed, and he growled, "I never fucking said that, baby girl. In fact, I'm very much missing those nails of yours on my skin. Do you even know how to use them anymore?"

His challenge had me itching to give him everything I knew he needed. I wanted to ride his cock and run my nails down his back and shoulders until his crimson blood spilled.

It took time to rebuild the trust between us, but I knew I was finally ready to accept him back into my body. To restore *that* connection now that our emotional one was back and stronger than ever.

The tension between us reached a boiling point, and I couldn't handle it anymore. I exploded forward, sealing our lips together as I pushed insistently at his shorts. My hand closed around his smooth cock, and I pumped up and down as I swallowed his groans.

He stepped out of his shorts before grabbing the hair at the nape of my neck and tugging it back to expose my throat, breaking off our heated kiss. I let out a small hiss at the pleasure-filled pain of his touch, and before I could think through my lustful thoughts, I *begged*.

"Drink from me."

A feral growl bubbled out of him in the second before he tore at my clothes, ripping my shirt away, peeling my pants off, and leaving me in only my thong and bra. As he grabbed my hips, I gasped, surprised and delighted by the weightless feeling in my stomach as he lifted me onto the cold marble countertop. He quickly dropped to his knees, burying his face between my legs.

My hands tangled in his messy hair as his fangs sank into the vein running up the inside of my thigh, and the sensation caused me to throw my head back with a cry of pleasure. It felt like shooting sparks of electricity traveled from the vein he punctured directly to the swollen and needy part of me that desperately wanted his attention.

I moved to brush my fingers over my clit, but he let out a growl as he tracked the movement out of the corner of his eye. He snatched my wrist and pulled it down to my side, refusing to let me relieve the ache building within me.

I'll be the one to bring you pleasure, baby girl. Until then, I want you writhing in need.

My entire body pulsated with need, and I let out a groan at his insistence on making me wait for relief.

His fingers skimmed up my other leg, lightly brushing up and over my knee toward my pussy, and my core tightened. The anticipation of his light touch and slow approach made a breathy sound of need fall from my lips as my hips rolled, trying to get him where I needed him.

Fuck. Please, Andrei. I fucking need you.

A deep chuckle came from him as he pulled his fangs from my leg, his lips bloodied with a drop trailing down his chin as he pinned me with a stare. "Tell me exactly what you want, baby girl." His mouth hovered over my thong, his hot breath teasing me alongside his fingers that skimmed the edge of the material. He demanded, "Tell me, and I'll give it to you."

Sexual frustration poured from me, making my body tense and aching with need. I practically threw my pussy toward his mouth, begging, "Please make me come, Andrei. I don't care if it's your fingers, tongue, or cock. Just make me come."

Silence descended as he brushed his fingers over my clit, not bothering to remove my underwear but honing in on the small bundle of nerves like a tracking beacon. "You don't care, huh?" he goaded, staring up at me with an expression I couldn't decipher. A mischievous one, perhaps, with a challenge lingering in his gaze.

He pushed up off his knees, leaving me gaping at him and panting with need.

"Well, then, I guess I haven't made enough of an impression with any of those options if you can't choose one you prefer."

He had to be joking.

"What are you doing?" I demanded breathlessly, jumping off the counter as he strode into the shower and began stroking his cock beneath the spray of water.

I stared at him, brain reeling from the way all of these men seemed to love edging me sexually.

I wasn't playing this game. I was going to get what was mine.

Ripping my bra and thong off, I padded in after him, loving the feel of the hot water as it cascaded over my body. Normally, it would relax me, but with the way I was wound up, the heat only served to make me aware of how sensitive my body felt to all stimulation.

As he reached for the loofah, I grabbed his arm. "Andrei! What the fuck? Why would you leave me hanging like that?"

He turned around so fucking slowly that the drops of water falling from the dark strands of hair hanging over his eyes drew my attention. Fuck me, the intensity pooling in his eyes reminded me of the way he stared down at me when I ran into his chest back on my first day at DIA.

My sharp inhale of breath echoed through the shower. My gentle mate was gone, replaced with a man who wanted to fucking *devour* me.

Andrei leaned against the wall as the water poured over his chiseled body, and my gaze fell slowly down, taking in all of him that glistened under the light. I gulped, staring at his cock straining in the air toward me, until his voice pulled my focus back up to his face.

"I know for a fact that you loved it when Drake ate your pussy in this shower right before Lincoln fucked you and spilled his seed into you," he purred, pushing off the wall to take a single step towards me. "Do you want me to call them in here so they can provide their tongue and cock for you? I know that was memorable enough for you to ask for it again."

His tone wasn't judgmental, so I didn't bristle at his words, but my brows rose in confusion as I stood my ground. "Is this all because I said I didn't care which part of you you used on me, Andrei? Seriously?"

I'd meant it in the best way possible because he was skilled with all three.

He was fast, but I easily tracked his movements as he grabbed my waist and pulled me to straddle him as he sat on the bench. My body rejoiced at the position, loving being near his cock, but as I tried to sink down onto his tip that brushed my entrance, his fingers dug into my hips. Stopping me.

I whimpered at being so damn close to what I needed once more but not being able to take it.

"Baby girl, don't say you don't care ever again because you fucking own me," he whispered before leaning forward to capture one of my nipples in his mouth, biting down hard enough to make the sensation feel like the most delicious of punishments.

I want to feel like I own you, too, body and heart.

"Fuck, yes..." I hissed as sparks of pleasure flowed from his rough touch.

My nails found his shoulders, and I dug the points of them in as my head fell back. The harsh bite to my nipple was quickly followed by soothing flicks of his tongue before he bit down with his fangs this time, eliciting a gasp from me.

I couldn't help myself—I tore my nails down his skin until I smelled the rich scent of his blood in the air.

Yes, baby girl. Mark me. Claim me.

He groaned against my breast as he drank from me, my core clenching as my body wound up toward the crest of an orgasm. Andrei played my body like a fine-tuned instrument.

Tell me, Alina. Tell me exactly what you want this time, and fucking mean it, baby girl.

I didn't think twice as I pulled my head back down to stare into his eyes. "I want your cock in me, Andrei. Now."

That's my good girl.

I was rewarded with him tugging my hips down as he thrust his cock into me all at once. I cried out, dragging my nails down his back as his hands trailed around to grab my ass, using his grip to help set the pace as I began to rock up and down on him.

He filled me thoroughly, stretching my body exactly the way I craved.

I was so worked up from the teasing that it only took a few hard thrusts before I was crying his name as I came. He didn't let up, though. Instead, he doubled down as he lifted me and swapped our spots, placing me on my hands and knees on the seat with my ass sticking up into the air.

He drove back into me without hesitation, the new position hitting a spot so deep inside of me that my hands curled into fists as the slapping sound of his skin against my body filled the space.

His hands rubbed over my bottom before he dug his fingers in. He was definitely an ass man.

A memory popped into my head with the realization of his obsession.

Do you remember what you said you wanted when Drake fucked me and played with my ass?

It had made me come so damn hard that I saw stars.

There was something about speaking so crassly about something that happened to me that had my pussy tightening around his cock, making him groan.

I sucked my bottom lip into my mouth and

nibbled on it as his words came to me, making my cheeks burn.

Yes, I said, I was going to enjoy watching your tits bounce as you rode me with my cock buried in your ass.

A mixture of hesitant nerves and a thrill of excitement ran through me. His pace slowed. His thrusts were deep, making my toes curl with each move.

His fingers trailed over my ass as he asked, "Are you saying you want to try it, baby girl?"

Maybe it was the delirious exhaustion rolling through me that influenced my risky decision, but I was quick to respond. After all, my body felt nothing but excitement about the prospect.

Yes, that's exactly what I'm saying, Andrei. Unless you no longer want it? I could call Drake to take care of that for me. He seemed quite keen to have me there.

My teasing words pulled the deep growl from him that I loved so much.

Don't. You. Fucking. Dare. Your ass is mine tonight.

CHAPTER NINE
ALINA

A cry puffed out of my lips as he pulled out of me, leaving me feeling bereft at the loss of his touch.

"Shhh, baby girl," he cooed, gathering me in his arms and nabbing a towel as he pulled us from the shower.

Crossing to my bedroom, he gently dropped me onto the bed after tossing the towel down. Not getting the bed soaked was a nice thought, but I had a feeling we wouldn't stay on the little rectangular piece of material.

I pushed onto my elbows as he crossed to my bedside dresser and pulled out a bottle of lube. Thinking we were going to pick up where we left off in the shower, I moved to turn over onto my hands and knees, but he was quick to stop me.

"No, baby," he purred as he dripped lube from the bottle over his cock before using his hand to cover every delectable inch of him. My eyes followed each stroke, heat coursing through my body. Fuck, I needed him back inside of me now. "You'll be on top—I said I wanted to watch you. It'll also give you a better position to take it at your pace."

I waited for him to join me on the bed, noting that as he laid down stroking his cock, he dropped the lube so it was near us. "Come here. I'm not done fucking your pussy yet," he purred.

Didn't have to tell me twice. My hearing was perfect—enhanced, even.

With utter enthusiasm, I straddled him and reached behind me to line him up with my entrance before sinking down. As I began to ride him, he pulled me down until our chests were pressed together. After a moment there, he moved until his upper body was angled to the side beneath me. I wanted to question what he was doing, but as I felt his lube-covered hand trailing over my ass, I knew. He was finding a good enough angle to be able to easily reach me to warm me up.

My body instinctively clenched as I slowed my rocking rhythm on his cock, but he was quick to jut his hips up, taking over and reigniting the desire within me. My pussy pulsed around him.

Relax, baby girl. You know I've got you.

I could finally say I did know that with all of my heart.

Taking a deep breath, I closed my eyes and remembered how great it felt when Drake played with my ass. On my exhale, I let all my muscles loosen, and Andrei slipped one finger in with ease, increasing the pace of his hips beneath me, giving me exactly what I needed to keep me focused on the good feelings.

A breathy sigh fell from my lips as he added a second finger and began pumping them in and out of me in tandem with the pace of his cock in my pussy.

"Shit," I groaned, still not used to this foreign sensation but pleasantly surprised by the way my body responded.

I winced slightly as he added a third finger, a pinching pain making me tense up and rethink whether this was something I would actually be able to follow through with. Thankfully, my pussy was so slick between the lube and my own arousal that, as he increased the pace to that of a frenzied madman, there was no pain left in my body. Only pleasure flowed through me as my eyes rolled back in my head and an orgasm ripped through me.

Without giving me a second to recover from the fuzzy orgasm tingles, he removed his fingers and helped me sit up straight as I lazily smiled down at him. Euphoria saturated every molecule of my body, which was exactly what I needed going into this.

I felt like I was having an out-of-body experience, floating in the clouds and only distantly hearing the lube bottle crack open as I pulled away from him and rose to my knees. It took a pinch on my nipple to draw me back to the present, but I moaned at the feeling as I looked down at Andrei.

"You still with me, baby?" he asked, a knowing smirk on his face as he rolled my nipple between his fingers.

"Mhm," I murmured, smirking back at him as I shuffled backward on my knees before dropping my hips down.

I kept my eyes on his, loving the way they smoldered with heat and gave me the encouragement I needed to do this. Grabbing his dick once more, I gently brought it up and pressed down very slowly until I felt the tip enter me.

His mouth popped open, and his eyes rolled back in his head as he groaned. The noises he was making spurred me on as his tip pressed inside the tight ring of muscles. My own mouth opened at the feeling as I sucked in a breath.

Shit.

It was a lot more to handle than his fingers in me, and I quickly bit down on my lips as a blossom of pain ripped through me. My body wanted me to stop—to pull him out—but he must have immediately felt it through our bond.

His hand moved to my clit, pressing down with his thumb and rubbing in circles that sent much-needed sparks of desire through me as his fingers on my breast began to roll my nipple and tug lightly.

Come on, baby girl, breathe. Let your body relax. Don't force it. Let yourself adjust before taking more.

His touch on my body, combined with his words, helped soothe the panic that had coiled in my chest from the pain.

Following his advice, I stopped trying to take more in, instead just letting my body adjust to his girth as he pulled one of my hands to my pussy, pressing my fingers down on my clit.

"You're allowed to touch yourself now, baby girl," he said softly, his eyes full of affection before turning into smoldering heat. "Show me what makes you feel good."

Now that I could definitely do.

You know what makes me feel good. You got a front-row seat from my dorm room window, or do you not remember?

Trailing my fingers softly over my clit as he reached for the lube once more, I increased the pressure and began to find the pace that forced a moan to bubble in my throat.

Andrei's eyes were glued to my movements as he poured some of the liquid onto his fingers without watching. After he tossed the lube away, he managed to tear his eyes from my fingers, flicking over my clit, bringing his own around to where our bodies met. I rose off of him so he could gently apply it to my entrance.

I promise you that memory will forever be ingrained in my brain, baby girl. It was the first time I'd ever seen a woman so brazenly confident in my life. Not to mention, it also gave me the worst case of blue balls I've ever had.

I couldn't hold back my small chuckle. *Damn straight.*

This time, as he helped guide it back into me, I lowered my hips further, taking him past the tip before pausing when I felt his shaft widen. Letting out a shaky breath, I continued to play with myself to keep my desire flowing through the discomfort. Andrei stared up at me, letting his eyes roam over every inch of me.

The fucking adoration sparking in his eyes could very well be my undoing.

You're so fucking beautiful, Alina.

His hands came up to cup my breasts, lavishing my nipples with attention.

Not just in the way your body is exquisitely stunning, but in the way your heart and tenacity shine through every day. The way you've proven to everyone around you what a force to be reckoned with you are.

His praise touched my heart *and* my pussy, making them both clench. I couldn't help but fuck with him back, though.

Are you giving me a pep talk to take your dick further in my ass?

Our joint chuckles floated through the air, making me feel at ease. His lips split into a full grin, and my heart rate increased at the way the simple move could transform his handsome features into ones that should be etched into statues.

Honestly, it should be illegal to have such a panty-melting smile.

I don't know—maybe. Is it working?

I didn't bother answering with words, feeling that my body was finally relaxing enough to take him in more.

With a quick mental pep talk of my own and a rock of my hips, he was finally buried within me. He let out a hiss, and I couldn't help but wonder if he was seeing stars right now.

I couldn't hold back. I threw his words back at him, a smirk pulling a corner of my lips up. "You still with me, baby?"

With a chuckle and a swat on my ass, he rolled his hips gently, moving into a new part of me that lay undiscovered before this moment.

Oh...*oh*. Now that I liked.

"Shit," I gasped, eyes wide as my fingers dug into his shoulders. "That feels amazing."

Gingerly, I rose up a bit before easing back down, finding a slow, rocking pace to start. A girl had to test the waters before letting her mate pound into her.

He pulled his bottom lip between his teeth, biting down as he flexed his hips up at the same moment I rocked down. The move had me whimpering, and my hands fell to his chest as he took over the rhythm.

Gradually, his pace increased until we were both a symphony of pants and moans, our bodies completely drowning in the incredible sensations.

"Fuck, baby girl," he groaned, his eyes closing like he was in bliss for a brief moment. "You're gripping me so fucking tight."

I felt the crest of my orgasm approaching lightning fast, and I bit my lip before crying out, "I'm so close, Andrei."

"Come on my cock, baby," he demanded, pounding into me over and over until I felt his own release coating my insides. It sent me over the edge, feeling his come marking me in this new place.

A force from within my core flowed through me, and I shattered. A rush of wetness came from my pussy, coating Andrei's stomach as he continued to languidly thrust into me through the pleasure, drawing out the orgasm as long as he could.

It wasn't very often I squirted, and a little embarrassment rolled through me at the way I had covered him in this position. I wanted to hide, my stomach twisting as I waited to see the disgust on his face.

Lifting myself off him, I fell to the side and grabbed a pillow to cover my face as I groaned. My words were muffled as I said, "I'm so sorry. I couldn't help it."

My fluffy shield was plucked from my hands and replaced with Andrei's face as he bent down and began peppering my face with little kisses. He didn't stop until I was giggling and pressing his chest to get him to stop.

Finally, he relented and pulled back enough to stare into my eyes. "There is absolutely nothing to be ashamed of or to be sorry for, baby girl. I love seeing the way your body reacts to me. There's nothing more satisfying."

The heat in my cheeks faded, and I gave a hesitant smile, my confidence bolstered by his words. "Are you sure?"

With a chaste kiss to my lips, he pushed up before dragging me with him. Tossing me over his shoulder like I was as light as a feather, he made the trek back to the bathroom as he smacked my ass.

"Absolutely. Don't ask again, or I'll be forced to make your body do it over and over again, forsaking the sleep I know you need right now."

Was sleep *really* that important?

Is that a threat or a promise? Unclear here.

With another smack to my ass, he set me down in the shower and offered me a stern look. "You and I both know your body needs to rest, baby girl."

With that, he grabbed my hips and shoved me underneath the water. Instantly, my body relaxed, enjoying the heat.

The time in the shower was utter bliss as we washed one another between long moments of kissing and holding each other. By the time he was toweling me off, though, the full weight of my exhaustion had hit me.

My body felt like jello, and my eyelids drooped. I was going to crash—hard. The days without sleep and extreme emotional turmoil were catching up with me now that I was thoroughly satisfied.

It hit me then that the bed was likely a mess from our time together, and I let out a groan as I walked toward the door. I quickly pulled to a stop at the threshold, though.

Lincoln was reclined on the freshly made bed, propped against the headboard, as he read a book shirtless. His head craned to look at me knowingly, and I shuffled from foot to foot under the weight of his gaze.

I took care of the clean-up, Princess. Come to bed.

A part of me still instinctively waited for them to be mad or jealous of each other when I had a moment alone with one, so the relief that flooded through me at his words was immense.

He was really fucking making an effort to show me he was in this with me and supporting every facet of this complicated relationship. There was no shame or guilt——just silent support as he ensured we'd have a place to rest together after I'd had my time with Andrei.

With a smile and a small slap to my ass from Andrei, who was waiting for me to move, I greedily crossed the distance before crawling up onto the bed. I waited for a moment as Lincoln dropped his book onto the nightstand. He lifted his arm for me after, and I cuddled up to his side, reveling in the heat of his body pressed against mine.

Andrei's warmth cocooned me from behind as he trailed soft kisses along the top of my shoulder.

Everything was close to perfect right now. You know, if I didn't think about the slayers and shit with them I still needed to deal with.

My mind searched for Drake. *Are you coming to*

bed soon, love? I know you're as exhausted as Lincoln and I are.

The weight of his emotions rolled through me—this overwhelming feeling of exhaustion, grief, and even his desire to be alone right now to process it all flowed through the bond openly.

I wanted to hold him in my arms.

I'm just handling the paperwork for the passing of the board members, Comoroă. I have to alert next of kin as well as handle a few other items. I'll come to bed as soon as I can. As much as they betrayed me, their loved ones still deserve to know about their passing so they can make arrangements to say goodbye. Also, as you know, Andrei handled the transport of Silvyn to the hospital while we were in Carmina, but I was just given a message that she was just put into hospice. The doctor said she's refusing to eat and likely won't make it.

Shit. In the frenzy of everything with Jeoffrey and Rin, followed by our harrowing journey to Carmina, the deaths of the other board members completely slipped my mind. I wasn't sure if that made me an awful person or not, considering I'd never had a relationship with them, but what I did know was that Drake was incredible. The way he balanced all his duties and roles was so admirable.

A part of me questioned whether I should go to him to support him through it, but I knew this was something he needed to do alone after feeling his needs through the bond. I had to respect those boundaries, and perhaps he needed to grieve in his own way. He'd lost people who had been around him for a long damn time, and betrayal like that ran deep.

It felt like a parallel issue I was going to face. Now that Lo was safe, there was nothing else to keep my thoughts from turning to House Devaroux.

I also had a hunch that he was struggling with Lo's decision to hang back with Oleander. As much as we had our own private time while living in the castle with her, there was an underlying warmth and joy to knowing she was just in the other wing. The castle felt a little less homey without her here.

I love you. You're a great friend, king, and mate.

His love poured through our bond. Contentment ran down my skin in a hot wave, making my heart beat a little faster. He truly loved me, all the way down to the darkest recesses of his soul.

Get some rest, Comoroă. I love you too.

My eyes fluttered closed on command as I snuggled further into the warmth of my mates beside me.

My last thought before sleep claimed me was one for Fate.

Whether it was fated or not, thank you for giving Lo back to us. My heart wouldn't have survived losing another family member.

CHAPTER TEN
ALINA

For once, no nightmares or dreams plagued me as I slept. It was just...quiet.

It was bliss for someone whose brain felt like it could never shut off. I was so jealous of the people who could fall asleep every night the second their head hit the pillow. Most nights, I was one of the lucky ones that got to spend a lot of quality time with my racing thoughts and anxiety as I stared up at the ceiling.

Rain pelted the windows of my room, sounding like a white noise that whispered to my brain to return to sleep.

A warm sensation between my legs had my eyes peeling open groggily. While my body seemed to be waking up, it was like my mind was reluctant to leave the void it'd comfortably fallen into. A spark of pleasure rose from my core, making my lips part as my blurry eyes tried to focus.

What the...?

The soft sound of rustling material met my ears, and as my eyes finally cleared enough to take in my surroundings. I saw a large figure beneath the sheets between my legs.

"Wha..." I started but was quickly silenced by my broody professor in my mind.

Close that pretty mouth, Princess. I don't want anyone else waking up. I want you to myself for a few moments while I have my breakfast.

Did he just say... Yup, he did. Fucking hell, that was probably one of the sexiest things he's ever said to me. Definitely on the top five list.

My eyes blinked rapidly on their own accord because I was most definitely not in charge of my body right now. Nope, not one bit.

I was mentally and physically a puddle for this man.

Risking turning my head both ways on my pillow to scout out our situation, I noted that Andrei was gone, but Drake was curled up on his side and facing me less than a foot away. Even in his sleep, he looked troubled, and I wanted to run my fingers along the crease between his furrowed brows, as if that could erase his problems.

I needed to check in with him today to see if there was anything I could do to help shoulder the burden he was feeling. He'd once told me that I no longer had any problems—*we* had problems, and I needed to make it clear to him that the sentiment went both ways. For now, I'd let him rest longer and try my damnedest not to wake him.

Heat traveled all the way from my navel toward my face. I was tempted to throw the sheets off to cool down, but decided that would actually only make the searing heat worse. At that point, I'd actually see Lincoln as he lifted my hips to the position he wanted his...breakfast in, and that would definitely make me a hell of a lot hotter.

As it was, I felt my legs trying to rub together to ease the ache pooling in me as I felt his shoulders settle against the bottom of my thighs. The softest growl sounded from him, despite his demand for me to be quiet. Apparently, it was only okay if he made noise.

Don't you dare close your legs to me. I'm fucking starving, Princess.

My mouth parted with a heavy intake of breath at those words.

Sorry, Sir.

His hands pried my legs all the way open as his mouth descended upon me. Divinus' pearly gates opened in my mind, and I swear I saw stars bursting to life before my eyes. With the first flick of his tongue over my clit, I had to quickly slap a hand over my mouth to muffle the cry that wanted to come out.

Holy shit. There was no way I was going to be able to stay quiet the whole time. Not with the sinfully wicked things he could do with his tongue. He was asking way too much of me.

My eyes were still trained on Drake, and although I knew he needed to sleep, I felt myself torn somewhere between wanting him to wake up and watch my pleasure and wanting to keep it between Lincoln and myself. On one hand, it felt ridiculously hot to be "sneaking around" at this moment, but I also knew that these two could make my body sing with pleasure when they shared me.

A soft growl came from Lincoln as he devoured me. His tongue was swirling, yet he somehow still sucked on my clit at the same time.

His enthusiasm was *everything*.

There was a distinct difference between someone who licked pussy because they felt obligated to and someone who had a burning desire within them to do it—and do it *right*. Whether it be to please themselves by way of their partner feeling pleasure or because they just loved the act of it.

And this man... He fucking loved it.

His tongue dove inside of me as his finger softly pinched my clit, pulling a small yelp from me before I could stifle it with my hand.

My heart rate increased to an all-time high as Drake's eyes slowly opened, pinning me with an intense stare as Lincoln continued to tongue-fuck my pussy.

Holy hell.

Instantly, I knew the answer to my earlier question. I most definitely wanted him to be awake, because the feeling of his eyes on me during this moment... It sent a new spiral of lust and desire flowing through me.

I bit my lip as Lincoln praised me.

You're so fucking wet for me, Princess.

I didn't want to tell him that Drake was awake. I couldn't give him any reason to stop because, as it was, I was already soaring towards an orgasm. Also, it was clear he was enjoying this little bubble of secrecy himself, and I didn't want to pop that.

The corners of Drake's lips tugged up into a

smirk as his eyes slowly traveled down to the hulking shape of a figure beneath the sheets. As he dragged them back up to me, his velvety-smooth voice flowed into my mind.

Well, good morning, Comoroă. I'd ask how your morning is going, but I think that's abundantly clear.

Yeah, I can't say that I have any complaints. It's a fine morning.

I was barely capable of keeping my mouth shut as Lincoln replaced his tongue with his fingers and moved his mouth back to my clit. My hips bucked as my eyes fluttered closed, and a loud moan escaped from my throat, despite my best efforts.

Shhh, Princess.

Drake held a finger up to his lips at the same time, which left my frazzled and lust-filled brain feeling ultra confused. He couldn't hear what Lincoln had said to me, so the timing was really ironic.

What a beautiful sight to wake up to, my treasure. Is Lincoln under the impression that he can have you all to himself this morning? If so, I'll be quiet and let him think that's the case while he gets his fill.

As Drake rolled closer to me, he let out a soft,

albeit fake, snore, causing Lincoln to growl into my mind as he paused in what he was doing.

Is that fucker awake?

My brain felt scrambled as my eyes tracked Drake. He was close enough now to move his head and arm without his body causing any noticeable movement on the bed. So as his mouth closed around my nipple closest to him and his hand fell to cup and knead my other breast, I did the first thing that came to mind and told a little white lie. I had to stealthily add a small barrier in my mind to Lincoln, hoping like hell he couldn't detect it.

Nope. Sound asleep. He just rolled closer in his sleep.

I wasn't sure how that nervous answer actually appeased him, but he blissfully returned to making my body feel like it was being destroyed in an inferno of desire, and I let out a small sigh of relief.

Somehow this had turned from what was initially me and Lincoln sneaking around next to Drake to Drake and me sneaking our own heated moment past Lincoln. My life was a whirlwind, and I was left with the breathtaking realization that I could never guess what was coming next. My men sure kept me on my toes, which happened to be curling at the moment from the sparks of pleasure shooting all over my body from their touches.

I had to take a deep breath and really, really concentrate to send a thought to Drake.

You have to block Lincoln from your mind if you want to get away with this.

He scoffed int my mind. ***I'm actually offended that you think I didn't do that already, Comoroă. What am I, a fledgling vampire with no control?***

There was no doubt he had more control over himself than anyone I'd ever met, vampire, slayer, or otherwise. Part of me really wanted to break that rigid control, though. I wanted his monster to come out and play with the dark parts of me that sought it out.

Show me how much control you have, then, I challenged. *Let your monster come out right now. Let him play.*

A rush of emotions flew through our bond as my back arched, feeling my orgasm fast approaching. Disbelief, fear, and intrigue were the main three emotions I could pick out from Drake.

I truly understood why he'd be fearful and doubtful of me wanting this. He'd shared with me the way he'd hurt people unintentionally in moments buried in the past. I trusted him, though, and he was mine. Every part of him was made for me, and that meant his monster too.

He pulled his head back to peer down at me, shaking it softly.

I...I don't think that's a good idea.

Please. Trust yourself, and trust me. Just because I don't have a physical way to pull my own monster to the surface doesn't mean I'm not hiding my own twisted, fucked-up version of myself deep down.

Our eyes locked as my mouth popped open, the wave of pleasure crashing closer and closer to cresting in my body.

Come for me, Princess. I want to feel your pussy convulsing on my fingers and tongue, and then I'm going to push you for another one before I've had my fill.

The command, hot and needy, was the last thing I needed to send me crashing. As my orgasm rolled through me, Drake's eyes flickered to black voids before flashing back to blue and then back to black, like he was struggling to give up control.

Trust in us.

I wasn't sure what it was that finally snapped within him, but as I felt myself floating in pleasure, my hips bucking from the sensitivity in my clit and Lincoln's unrelenting touch, his eyes finally fully turned into the black void and stayed that way.

The tips of his fingers lengthened into the now-familiar black claws, dragging over the sensitive skin of my breast. I sucked my lip between my teeth, biting down against the urge to moan loudly at the sight of the veins running under his eyes and up his hands.

Having this side of him meant everything to me. It felt like the last barrier that stood between us was crumbling.

My pussy clenched in response to the monster writhing to the surface of his consciousness through our bond, and I let my lip pop from between my teeth. A small whimper escaped me as his mouth descended and crashed against mine. Our tongues clashed in an instant flurry, and I knew instinctively that we were fighting for dominance.

There was nothing soft and sensual about it. No, it was animalistic and raw.

The dark part of my soul wanted to show him that I could handle all of him. I could take everything he gave me, regardless of the form he gave himself to me in.

The bond between us seemed to be...closing, as if he didn't want me in his mind during this moment, despite letting his monster come out to play with me physically.

Don't you fucking dare, I snapped. *You better give*

me all of you, Drake. Don't offend me by thinking I can't handle it.

And just like that, it was like he snapped his fingers and opened the floodgates. My breath was stolen from my lungs to feel him in this way for the first time. Everything felt deeper and more…barbaric.

Drake was a very emotionally in-tune man, but this side of him had only thoughts of how badly he wanted to have me coming on his cock. The desire to watch my body writhe as I struggled beneath the darkness it wanted to pulse into me.

Lincoln pushed another finger into me, stretching me and making my hips rock as I tried to find the pace and rhythm I so desperately wanted.

You get to come when I allow it, Princess.

My body stilled instantly, though not just because of Lincoln's command. No, what I felt from Drake had my body wanting to submit. A part of me knew that he was now above me on the food chain, no matter my skills or abilities with my soul weapon.

This version of Drake could tear me limb from limb, and it caused a shiver of need to flow through me straight to my throbbing clit.

I felt the sharp thought of wanting to wrap his

darkness around my throat until my eyes fluttered, and the dark part deep inside of me purred in response. Typically, Lincoln was the only one who took that control from me, but I knew this wouldn't be the same.

Give it to me, I demanded. *I can handle it. I want it.*

He sucked my tongue into his mouth and used his fangs to nick my tongue, the taste of copper filling my mouth.

My throat began to constrict, and my mind raced as to how that was possible when I could feel one hand on my breast and the other trapped beneath him with the way he laid on his side to face me.

Was this his darkness at work? The black veins I'd seen beneath his skin as his monster surged to the surface?

My eyes bulged, and an instinctive sense of acceptance came over me, urging me to fight the fear at the loss of control as a deeper voice than I was used to hearing spoke to me, making me freeze. It was still Drake, but not—he had a much deeper and gravellier tone, like he'd gargled glass.

Submit, Precious.

Precious? Similar to treasure, I suppose, but still distinctly different from my usual nickname.

So *this* was his monster.

It wasn't that his monster was a separate entity because I could still feel Drake within the connection, but the depth of it was like a corner of his soul I'd yet to connect to and explore.

Let me make you feel good. I can give you that with my power. I know you can take it. Your own darkness calls to mine. You are a mirror of myself.

A cold, tingling sensation swooped around my neck and down to my breast. Pinpricks of pain and pleasure rolled just under the surface of my skin as more pressure was applied to my neck.

I didn't understand it, but I realized I didn't need to. I trusted him to take me where I wanted to go and to ensure I was safe while doing it.

As Lincoln's pace began to increase within me and the lapping of his tongue on my clit turned into long, hard strokes that had me soaring again, I found my moan caught in my throat. I was entirely unable to let any noise or air out.

My nipples pricked, and my chest heaved with the need to breathe.

A fresh wave of wetness coated Lincoln's fingers, and he let out a soft growl between my legs. The sound made Drake's eyes snap to him as he lifted his head from me, narrowing to slits.

Focus on me, I coaxed him, feeling his thoughts suddenly turn territorial. *Make me come.*

Black dots began to dance in my vision, the bliss of losing control flooding my brain with serotonin.

Yes. This was *everything.*

I feel you squeezing me, Princess. Do you want to come?

Fuck yes, please, I practically cried back.

The muscles in my abdomen clenched in response to the way they were holding my body in a void between pleasure and pain. Maybe it was fucked to crave this type of passion, but this was me, and Fate knew what she was doing. She gave me mates who could give me everything I wanted and never make me feel shame for it.

Lincoln's fingers curled inside me, hitting a spot that had my hips straining. His arm moved to press across my lower stomach to keep me down, and his tongue increased in pressure as he stoked the fire within me.

Drake's gaze fell back to me, the dark voids calling to my soul as my vision began to blur.

Come for me, Precious. I want to savor this moment together while I can.

Come for me, Princess.

Their demands were simultaneous, and I

couldn't contain myself anymore. The grip on my throat loosened as I let out my cry of release. It felt like my entire body spasmed from the sensory overload, and despite having the ability to suck in deep lungfuls of oxygen again, I struggled around my screams.

Lincoln pulled the covers from my waist until he was able to pop up and stare at me in satisfaction. His contented smile vanished the second he saw Drake lazily smirking at him with a finger waggle in his direction.

"I thought you said he was asleep?"

His angry words were directed at me, but I was too lost in bliss to defend myself.

CHAPTER ELEVEN
ANDREI

Nerves fluttered in my stomach as my footsteps on the hard floor echoed across the vaulted ceilings, somehow reminding me that I was nearing a momentous occasion in a place that had very quickly morphed into a place of peace and refuge for me.

I was going to introduce Alina to my mother today.

Just the thought of it made my chest coil with a mixture of fear and anticipation. Suddenly, my throat felt tight and uncomfortable as I tried to swallow down the emotion.

I wasn't sure how it would go between them, but it was important to me for the two women I loved most in this world to meet. Especially now that my mother was no longer under Jeoffrey's control.

I refused to even call him my father. All he represented was a sick monster who controlled people around him through violence and manipulation. When Alina destroyed him, it felt like the little boy in me could finally breathe a sigh of relief. I didn't have to keep searching for a sliver of humanity within Jeoffrey that might redeem him or bring me closer to having a real father.

My lips tilted up in a smile to myself as I remembered the way my mom reacted when she'd become lucid again, and I told her that he was out of our lives. For good. A small shred of happiness had reflected back at me in her eyes, and it was the first time I'd seen it in too long to even remember.

I knew this was the perfect time to introduce them before we were off again to fight yet another battle.

Raising my hand to rap my knuckles against Alina's door, I paused at the sound of squabbling from inside.

"You can't let me have a single moment alone with her, can you?"

"You can't expect me to not join when I see her

writhing with need before me, brother. Come now. That's a ridiculous question."

Dropping my hand to my side, I let out a heavy sigh and shook my head. Honestly, I didn't think I would ever understand Drake and Lincoln's relationship. At times, they seemed to operate under a friendly cease-fire and were more than happy to share her when it came to punishing me. But then, out of nowhere, they'd get territorial again. To top it all off, Drake was now calling him *brother*. I just couldn't keep up with them.

Not bothering to knock, I pushed the door open and walked a few feet in before leaning against the wall, taking in the scene. Alina was lying on the bed like a wet noodle, completely melting into the mattress. The sleepy smile on her face let me know she was definitely in her post-orgasm state, and their argument wasn't bothering her in the least.

Arguably, this was my favorite version of her. It was so rare to see her relaxed enough to not be worrying about the inevitable next life-changing problem we had to face.

My cock twitched at the sight of her naked body, but I quickly doused the idea of taking her in the shower. I wasn't sure what they'd done with her so far this morning, but I knew from last night alone that she was probably going to feel tender. She deserved time to recover.

Crossing my arms over my chest, I cleared my throat to get their attention. "If you guys want to continue this, please, be my guest. However, I'm taking Alina this morning, so if you could take this somewhere else so she can get ready, that would be great."

Lincoln and Drake's heads snapped toward me at the same time, twin expressions of annoyance on their faces. Both stared at me with narrowed eyes and thin lips, their expressions speaking volumes of what they thought of my plan. Good thing I didn't give a fuck what they thought.

Thankfully, Alina seemed to come out of her orgasmic state at my announcement, popping up and crawling out of bed before they could grab her to keep her between them.

They let out echoed grumbles as she tugged a black robe on, hastily tying the waistband before padding up to me. Opening my arms, I loved the way she melded herself to my front, snuggling against my chest as I dropped my chin to rest on her head.

That's my baby girl.

Her voice was muffled against my chest as she asked, "What are we doing?"

Those damned anxious flutters hit me hard again, my throat fighting my ability to get the words out to answer her. Eventually, I managed to croak, "I thought you could maybe...truly meet my mom today."

A small gasp came from her as she pulled back to stare up at me with wide, searching eyes. "Really? Is she feeling up to it?"

I could sense her nerves but also a bit of excitement. Relief flowed through me, and I rubbed my hand along her back, smiling like an idiot that she was open to it. I knew without a doubt that there was no forcing Alina Van Helsing to do anything she didn't want to do, so her agreement was a vital part of the equation.

"Yes, baby girl," I answered before turning her around and giving her a smack on the ass, which was quickly turning into my new favorite thing. "So go take a quick shower and get dressed unless you want her to smell the orgasm on you."

She gasped and ran like her ass was on fire, pulling a soft chuckle from me. Drake and Lincoln quickly diffused themselves the moment she was out of the bedroom, and with comments about where they could be found today if we needed them, they were off. I stood next to the large windows, watching the rain fall on this dreary day as I waited for her.

She didn't leave me waiting for long. Alina had never been the type to spend long getting ready, but she still somehow managed to look like the most beautiful woman I'd ever laid my eyes on, no matter what version of her I got.

Cranky Alina—stunning and adorable with the way her brows furrowed.

Turned on Alina—ridiculously appealing with the way her pupils turned to little pricks and breath fanned over her parted, beautiful lips.

Angry Alina—breathtaking with the way her fire burned so brightly within her, always with a determined set to her shoulders and a tilted chin as she dared anyone to get in her way.

Sleepy Alina—heart-warming with the absolute cuddle puddle she turned into, seemingly wanting to inhale us with the way she clung to and wrapped herself around us.

As she crossed the room to me, a nervous energy radiating through our bond, I couldn't help but reach out to caress her cheek before leaning down to seal our lips together. Every time I felt the warmth of her skin on mine, a small piece of my damaged heart began to heal.

I knew it wasn't her job to make me whole again. It was my responsibility to do the work to continue to heal myself, but damn if she didn't give me the love I had always craved but never knew I needed.

Giving her plush bottom lip a small nip before backing up, I drank in the flush spreading over her cheeks as her damn pupils dilated, signaling exactly how she felt at the moment.

"What was that for?" she asked breathlessly, threading our hands together as she stared up at me.

It was such a simple question, but it didn't have a simple answer.

Squeezing our joined hands, I inhaled deeply and let my chest expand until I blew all the air out with a shaky chuckle. "To put it simply, Alina, it's for everything. Everything you are. Everything we are. Everything we will become with time. I knew you were mine, even when the odds weren't in our favor. I can't imagine how much more my love for you will grow in the future, but with every passing day, it grows larger. A few years from now—shit, fifty years from now—I feel like I'll die from the love bursting out of my heart for you."

I sucked in another deep breath, chest heaving after word vomiting with no breath in between.

Her eyes brimmed with unshed tears as she smiled up at me, squeezing my hand back. "Shit, how am I supposed to follow that up? You have a way with words that I'll never have."

Lifting one hand to brush my lips against her knuckles, I looked at her from beneath my lashes and murmured, "You don't need to put it into words, baby girl. I feel your love in your actions and through our bond every day."

I love you.

I love you too.

After we both gathered ourselves, I tucked her against my side and guided us toward the room I'd set my mother up in near the entrance to the castle. It was far enough away in the large building that I didn't fear her hearing our activities or conversations, but close enough that I could be there for her if she needed anything.

We were there in no time, and I knocked on the heavy wooden door as Alina shifted her weight from foot to foot anxiously beside me.

"Come in!" Mom called out, followed by the clinking of what sounded like glass.

Pushing the door open, I found her nervously

moving around cups of tea on the small sitting table at the far side of her room, near the corner window. The natural light illuminated the pale tone she'd taken on while I was away at school, and she was left alone with Jeoffrey. The way she had withered to nothing more than skin and bones, it seemed like she had stopped going outside and feeding properly. Even her hair looked brittle, lacking a healthy shine.

For a fleeting moment, I felt a sense of nerves at the thought of Alina taking her in fully while she was in this state. My mom hadn't always looked like this, and I hoped that with her newfound freedom, she could get back to a healthy state.

Alina didn't miss a beat, though, letting go of my hand to cross the room. I should have known she wouldn't blink twice at my mom's appearance. Alina knew exactly what my mother had endured.

"Is it okay if I give you a hug?" my mate asked in a timid voice that I don't think I've ever heard her use before.

My mom startled, her mouth popping up and her green eyes flicking back and forth between Alina and me. From our earlier conversations, I knew the thought of Alina judging her for her actions, or lack thereof, when it came to me was eating away at her.

Smoothing her hands over the plain white dress

a staff member had picked up for her, she swallowed hard. "I...I would love that."

What started as a gentle hug between them quickly turned into a squeezing embrace, like they were holding each other together. My throat constricted at the sight, and my eyes burned as I forced myself to take deep breaths to try not to let the emotion of the moment overcome me.

Apparently, I wasn't the only one plagued with overwhelming emotions. My mom's body shook as Alina held her tightly, her sniffles audible through the quiet room.

"I'm s-so s-s-orry...I d-idn't p-p-protect him more," she sobbed, her voice trembling so much that I wasn't sure if Alina could even understand her. She took a shaky, deep breath, and her next words came out a bit more clear. "I failed as his mother and was the reason you two were torn apart from each other. It's all my fault. I should have left when he was a baby."

Fury roared to life in my chest, my hatred for Jeoffrey rekindling all over again because he'd ever made her feel like this. I never once thought of her as a failure.

Alina rubbed soothing circles over her back, easily tucking her head on top of my mother's as she curled her larger frame around her. "You did every-thing you could, Serena. You both managed to stay alive under the control of that manipulative son of a bitch." Her eyes met mine, and I knew her next words were meant for both my mother and me as she said, "You aren't a failure. You're a survivor, and I think that makes you incredibly strong."

Yup, there was no holding back the tears that demanded to fall from my eyes. Wetness coated my cheeks, and I didn't even bother to wipe it away, knowing more would come.

My mother's hands trembled as they moved to grip Alina's arms lightly, parting just enough to look up at her. "Di...did you kill him?"

Shock slammed into me. She hadn't asked me for details when she woke up, and I told her he was gone for good.

Alina's eyes shifted to mine, and I felt her nerves through the bond. She didn't want to step on any toes, and I appreciated her concern.

You can tell her. I don't think she remembers what happened when she was drugged. When she woke up, all I had to tell her was that he was gone for good, and that seemed to be good enough for her.

With a small nod, she focused back on my mom and took a deep breath before exhaling quickly. Her own voice was a little shaky, though it shored up as she spoke. "I did. Andrei asked me to do it, and I was more than willing to rid this earth of that monster."

For a moment, they simply stared at each other, and the energy in the room filled with nervous tension as I held my breath, waiting for her reaction.

Fresh tears fell over my mom's cheeks as she closed her eyes and whispered, "Thank you."

The release of emotions that seemed to come from my mom with those two words was immense. Her entire body relaxed, sagging back into a chair with Alina's assistance, which was substantial.

It was a moment I'd forever hold close to my heart as I watched it truly wash through my mom.

I rushed to her side, kneeling next to the chair as I gently grabbed her hand. Alina took the seat to her left, holding her other hand. My mate's eyes held so much sympathy and compassion, and I knew this was one of those moments where my love for her was growing so fucking much that I was shocked that I was even able to hold it all within me.

"He's dead..." my mom whispered, trailing off and shaking her head in disbelief as she stared at the table holding the tea. "He's never going to hurt us again."

This was what I'd always dreamed of but feared

would never come true. We truly were free to live our lives without the fear of Jeoffrey every day.

"Never again," I echoed, another tear rolling down my face as I tried to smile at Alina.

The gift she'd given us with Jeoffrey's death was one that couldn't ever be put into words.

CHAPTER TWELVE
ALINA

My heart felt raw, yet somehow still full as we wrapped up our visit with Serena. As a survivor in my own way, I felt a kinship with her, and I desperately wanted to spark the confidence within her that I knew she once had. I wanted to see her joy return to her and for her to find a purpose in life that went beyond merely getting through every day.

You didn't survive a life of abuse without fostering an ember of strength, tenacity and a little bit of stubbornness, too, to carry on every day.

As we held each other in a goodbye hug with the promise of having tea again soon, I felt reluctant to let her go. As we got to know each other over the course of our visit, I watched her slowly begin to come back to life. There were flashes of small things, like the way her shoulders rolled back, and she stopped averting her eyes when we engaged in conversation about herself. Her voice had eventually gotten a little stronger, no longer trembling once she accepted the truth of Jeoffrey's death.

I had no doubt that before Jeoffrey warped her into this fragile shell of the person she'd become, she was a strong-willed and determined woman. What she survived took a type of strength that no one would ever understand without being in the same position themselves. I wanted to help that ember of strength, determination, and grit explode outward until she was rising anew.

I was worried that if we left her alone, she would sink back into the shell that had become her everyday normal. Those habits, learned from years of abuse, weren't things you could easily break.

"It was so lovely meeting you properly, Alina," she said as we finally let go, and I stepped into Andrei's outstretched arm. Serena's eyes misted with tears again, gazing adoringly at Andrei for a few seconds before giving me her focus once more. "I couldn't have chosen a more perfect mate for my son. I look forward to watching your love continue to blossom."

Andrei's hand rubbed up and down the outside of my arm, his affection for both his mother and me ringing loud and clear through our bond.

All I could do was smile at her and return the sentiment of it being great to meet her, honestly feeling a bit choked up in an unexpected way. Andrei steered us out of the room, and I couldn't help but glance over my shoulder at her, finding her smiling at us. A motherly warmth exuded from her, and I was hit with the realization that it was the one part of her that could never be suppressed by anyone—not even Jeoffrey, from the way Andrei spoke of her love for him as he grew up. It poured through, from her words to her touch and even the way she looked at him.

My own mother's face flashed through my mind, and I winced, taking in a sharp inhale of breath.

It made me miss her really fucking bad. I quickly whipped my head back around to face where we were going. I hated that a part of me wanted to cling to Serena to simply fill that empty hole in my life. It wasn't fair of me to expect that from her—especially after what she'd been through—and it wasn't fair to think even for a second that anyone could fill my mother's shoes.

Are you okay, baby girl? Andrei asked, glancing down at me as we walked, concern coating his tone.

Shockingly, my first instinct was to respond to him and tell him everything, but I quickly swallowed the truth when I realized the can of worms it would open. It wasn't just this one question. It was all the trauma attached to it, and this was not a road I could go down right now or anytime soon. I needed to keep my shit together just a bit longer.

I took a deep breath and cleared my throat before forcing a tight smile onto my face as I looked up at him. I didn't trust myself to respond, so I just nodded before dropping my head back down.

His unease skittered through our bond, but I threw up a wall over the raw emotions churning within me. I *couldn't* go there. I'd meticulously suppressed everything over the past few weeks, and I refused to let it all crumble and tumble out now in a weak moment.

I thought I'd managed to seal the gaping hole within my chest with cement since my family's death, but being around Serena was blowing it wide the fuck open. There was something about the warm embrace of a maternal figure that apparently had me wanting to crawl into her lap and tell her how fucking hard life had been lately.

I nibbled on my lip at the idea, hating the way I couldn't just let it go, despite trying to force myself to repeatedly in the past hour. How fucked up did that make me? I hadn't even properly allowed myself to mourn my family, and here I was, jumping to plug the hole in my heart with someone else instead.

I suddenly felt very, very weak at the inability to bottle up these tumultuous emotions.

My brow furrowed as we walked into the kitchen, and I quickly grabbed a seat on a bar stool as Andrei grabbed us some blood from the fridge.

"I'm so happy to see how well you both got along," he called out, digging around to find the proper bags for each of us. "When do you think you'll want to see her again? Name it, and I'll arrange it."

My eyes snapped shut as I curled my fingers into tight fists in my lap, taking a deep breath at his question and the way my heart soared at the thought. Traitorous little organ.

You have to stay away from her until this is done, Alina. You can't afford cracks in the foundation right now.

I had a feeling it would only get harder to resist opening up to her as she healed. If I already had the urge to confide in her, I couldn't imagine the way my soul would yearn for it when she found herself again. No part of me wanted to feel like a burden when she was fighting so hard for herself right now.

"I think it's best to wait for all of our problems with our enemies to be solved before I see her again," I responded tightly, forcing my eyes back open as I heard his feet shuffle. "There's a lot on our plates, and I don't want her to have to be worried about us."

I knew she'd never be the person she was before Jeoffrey. That version of her had suffered for years and years, dying at the hands of an abusive mate. Trauma lingered in one's soul, impacting everyday choices and even the subconscious thoughts people have about themselves and the people around them. It was a stain that could never be removed, but we could learn how to find the new version of ourselves that was born during those defining moments.

I knew because *I* was learning how to find that new version of myself.

"You're going to chew your own lip off if you keep gnawing on it like that," Andrei states with a raised eyebrow on his approach, dropping my usual bags in front of me and pulling me from my tumultuous thoughts. "If you change your mind about wanting to see her sooner, let me know—I know she'd love it."

His tone was dejected, empty of the joy that had clung to his words after meeting Serena.

Now I felt guilty as fuck.

A sharp puff of air passed through my nostrils as my eyebrows raised, pushing away the ugly thoughts that festered all the way down to my soul. "I'll think about it."

My hands shook slightly as I grabbed my blood bags and unscrewed the caps.

Fuck, keep it together, Alina.

It's okay to not be okay.

My lip curled at Dev's words, but I raised the bag and started sucking down my blood to hide the reaction from Andrei.

I don't have time to not be okay.

Andrei's hand dropped onto my shoulder, squeezing gently. I took strength in his steady, grounded presence as I thought back to the woman I was the first day I came to DIA. I'd grown so much since then, and I needed to celebrate that.

Besides, the only way I got to this point was by suppressing everything to the deepest, unreachable levels within me. It was really fucking hard and took effort every single day, but I came closer to letting go of my old life with each passing second. I wanted to be done with it. To shed that version of myself once and for all, as well as all the issues that came along with it.

Maybe if I could do that, I'd never have to fully face the skeletons piled up in my closet.

Andrei's hand fell away from my shoulder, and I missed his grounding warmth as he went to tinker with the coffee machine. I stared at his back, zoning out a bit as I scowled at the realization that there was only one thing holding me back from finally letting that version of me go once and for all.

Anger coursed through me at the thought of Jade and her family, and I fully welcomed it into my body and mind. This was an emotion I was comfortable with—like an old, familiar friend.

Sparks of determination flooded me as I clenched my hands tightly at the thought of ripping their throats out. I breathed the hatred in. *This* was something I could use. My thirst for vengeance would consume me and keep the unwanted memories at bay.

I wouldn't feel peace until I handled this final hurdle, and my soul desperately needed to be free of the shackles weighing it down.

It was time to actually finish my blood oath and

take them down.

I sent out a mental call to Lincoln and Drake to meet us in the conference room, refusing to answer their questions about what the summoning was regarding. Instead, I told them they'd find out when they got there.

Jumping off the stool, I deposited my empty bags in the stainless steel trash can and snagged the coffee Andrei had poured for me in my designated mug. It was black and had two tiny, white baby fangs on it. It was cutesy, and I secretly fucking loved it.

Andrei was quick to grab my arm, dragging me to a stop before I could get far.

I knew he wasn't going to let my broody mood go, but I had been hoping I could hold him off until we were all together in the conference room.

"What's bothering you, Alina?" he asked, sounding somehow wounded by my current disposition. "I know that was an emotional meeting with my mom, and I'm sorry if it upset you."

Shit, now I feel awful. Of course, he assumed the way I walled off my emotions and thoughts from him, so he didn't hear my turmoil, was because of the conversation with his mom. My trauma was something I wanted to process alone, and I hadn't for a second thought about how it would appear to him after meeting her.

Sometimes I really felt like a shitty mate to these incredible men.

With a heavy sigh, I faced him and pressed up onto my tiptoes to kiss his cheek. "I'm sorry. It isn't about your mom, I promise. I genuinely adored getting to know her." Before he could respond or pry about my mood, I dropped onto my heels and said, "Lincoln and Drake are meeting us in the conference room. I promise my mood has everything to do with my own shit. I'll explain as soon as we're all together, okay?"

His eyes were guarded, and I felt him probing at my mind, but my shield was solid. As soon as he felt the shield, his lips turned down into a frown, and pain leaked into his voice as he asked, "Why do you have a wall up between us?"

"I..." I started but trailed off when I realized I was at a loss for words.

How did I explain that this was my trauma response—that guarding myself from anyone knowing of my weak and vulnerable sides made me feel the safest?

I loved and trusted my three mates, but there was still a knee-jerk reaction to not letting those parts of me be seen. I'd been raised with the ideology that you should not let anyone know your weakness for fear of it being used against you. If you convinced your own mind that you were fine, your enemies would never be able to hit you where it hurt the most. Maybe it was unhealthy to have such a cold method of detachment, but it was my coping mechanism, and that wasn't going to change overnight.

Without waiting for me to finish, he relented, dropping his hand from my arm. He turned away from me, focusing on adding sugar to his coffee. "Okay, I'll wait."

Relief flooded through me at not being forced to hash this out with him right now, just when I'd have to do it all over again with Drake and Lincoln in the conference room. I also desperately needed a few more minutes to gather my erratic thoughts. It stung to hear the sharp tone in his voice, though.

He was my more sensitive mate, and he was absolutely taking my current state personally. I shook my head softly at the thought. I couldn't blame him. I'd feel the same way if the roles were reversed, but I couldn't soften now. I was already teetering too close to the edge after my emotional morning.

Words were hard right now, but I knew I could show him my gratitude in a different way.

"Thank you," I whispered, forcing my bond back open with him so he could feel the depths of my feelings in that specific matter, despite my inability to form the words right now.

It was enough to earn a small smile from him, and as soon as I felt like he was okay, I focused once more on Jade and her family.

I mentally dumped gasoline on the ember of hatred festering within me, remembering the times our families had dinner together. The way they'd openly supported our family and smiled to our faces. The way Jade had wormed her way into my heart from such a young age.

How long had their plan been in the making?

Were our ten-plus years of friendship all a sham?

My eyes fluttered closed as I wrapped myself in the blanket of betrayal that allowed my mind to feel sharp and focused on my mission.

When I felt centered and ready for what came next, my eyes snapped back open, at peace with how I needed to conduct myself.

I wasn't going to let anything distract or stop me from getting my vengeance now.

CHAPTER THIRTEEN
ALINA

I let out a heavy sigh as we settled into the uncomfortable chairs in the conference room. Lifting my coffee up to take a gulp of the hot liquid, I moan, enjoying the burning trail it left down my throat and into my chest.

After placing the cup back down, I tapped my feet impatiently against the stone floor, hoping Lincoln and Drake would show up soon. Andrei was definitely giving me the space I'd silently asked for, but it felt like there was a gaping chasm opening with the physical distance he'd put between us.

I needed to keep my distance from them all until there were solid plans in place. At first, I thought Serena was what put a crack in my foundation, but as I studied Andrei's handsome face, I felt my heart lurch. The truth was that my mates were slowly chipping away at the stone front I'd worked so damn hard to construct ever since I left my home and went to DIA with Estrid.

They'd each chipped away at those layers, helping me become a better woman, friend, and mate in the process. But I couldn't afford to continue to allow my heart to be as exposed as I'd come to realize it now was.

You do know that the emotions you're hating on so hard right now are what kept you from hurting anyone else after Skye, right? They're what allowed you to have such control over yourself, despite being a fledgling vampire, when you should have been lost to the bloodlust overcoming you in your early stage.

My brow pinched together as my lips tightened, fury pouring through me at Dev even bringing Skye up.

Don't you dare talk about her!

No—you may be able to boss around everyone else, but I won't allow you to do it to me. I have been so proud of the way you have embraced the path your heart and feelings have taken you down recently. Why would you throw it all away now to return to the slayer you used to be?

Andrei's eyes flicked to me as if he could sense the annoyance within me, and I lifted the coffee back up to my lips to avoid having to answer the lingering question and concern in his gaze.

There is no choice with the path that lies ahead of me. I won't be able to complete my blood oath if I let my feelings control me.

Have you ever stopped for a moment to think about why that may be? Maybe that path doesn't serve you anymore.

I drained my coffee before slamming the mug onto the table a little too hard.

If I wanted a therapy session, I'd give my old friend Vic a call.

Drake and Lincoln arrived at that very moment, saving me from the wretched conversation with Dev. I gave them each a tight smile as they dropped kisses on my cheeks before settling into chairs on either side of me.

"What's going on, *Comoroă?*" Drake asked, wasting no time as he rubbed a hand over the stubble growing on his jaw.

I took a deep breath, preparing to lay it all out there, but I found myself a bit tongue-tied on where to even begin. My eyes darted around between their concerned faces before finally landing on the surface of the table. It felt a hell of a lot easier not to meet their eyes right now.

Why did I suddenly feel so nervous with all of their gazes on me? They'd always supported me in getting justice for the deaths of my family. My desire to continue on that path now wouldn't be shocking news.

Just rip the fucking Band-Aid off, Alina.

My eyes fell closed for a brief second as I took a deep, centering breath.

Remember who the fuck you are. Alina Van Helsing.

Tilting my chin up and drawing my shoulders back, I met each of their eyes before stating, "I want to make plans on how to tackle the threat of Jade's family being in charge of the slayers. If Jeoffrey was telling the truth about their hand in my family's demise, I know they won't stop at the power they hold now. We need to prepare ourselves, and our people here in Sanguis, for when they break the laws we've established. And I still want justice for my family."

I expected them to jump right into planning with me, but I was instead met with silence as the three of them exchanged looks. No doubt they were talking to each other and excluding me, which was rude as hell, considering I was right fucking here.

I let it go on for a few seconds before I'd had enough. The blood in my veins felt like it was boiling under my skin from my anger. I would not be excluded by my mates from a conversation that I'd initiated, and that meant so much to me.

A growl slipped from my throat, and I smacked the table with my palm as I lurched to my feet. "If you have something to say, say it to me."

I thought you were going to keep your emotions under wraps. Or does that only apply to specific ones?

The tips of my fingers pressed into the hard wood of the tabletop as I fought to keep from balling my hands into fists and punching a hole through the damn thing.

I glanced at Andrei first, and he at least had the decency to look sheepish. The two dickheads on each side of me didn't look repentant at all. Lincoln crossed his arms over his chest and raised an eyebrow at me. "Sit down, *Princess*."

Oh, hell no.

Using *that* nickname with *that* inflection was the absolute wrong thing to do. It only lit a fire under my ass that pulled a deep laugh from my chest as I smiled patronizingly back at him. "We're not in your class, *Sir*, and even if we were, we both know I'm not keen to listen to demands."

I didn't give him a moment to rebut, asking instead, "Why the hell are you all not jumping at the chance to help me? I have been so painstakingly open with you about how much my blood oath means to me. I need it *done*."

My body began to shake, the betrayal coursing through me like poison.

"That is not what is going on," Drake snapped. "We simply all agree that you should take longer than one day off from your vendetta, Alina. We have all been run ragged with everything going on non-stop lately. Physically and emotionally."

My head jerked back at his words, a huff of air passing through my nostrils. I looked around at each of them, waiting for them to backtrack, but they didn't.

So, they all agreed with that, then.

"Well, if that's how you all feel, you're more than welcome to sit back and relax while I continue to push on," I whispered quietly, the heartbreak of realizing they'd made this decision without me breaking through my haze of anger.

I wasn't sure how I would manage it alone. I'd

come to rely on their help, and maybe that was my first mistake.

My chest deflated as I kicked the heavy chair back and turned, ready to get away from all the feelings of hurt, betrayal, and anger swirling through me. I needed a moment to process this alone.

"Don't you dare walk out that door, Alina," Lincoln commanded, the screech of his chair being pushed back behind me, raising my hackles. "Don't walk away from us and your problems. Not again."

I felt Drake's eyes boring into my face from the side—I hadn't quite made it past him in my desire to get the hell out of this room. I ignored him. But Lincoln's words pressed a button within me that made me snap.

Whirling around until I faced him, my eyes narrowed on the man that I thought would love me to the end of our days. Acid dripped from my every word as I clipped back, "Walk away from my problems? I'm trying to fucking face them head-on right now, and none of you want to help me!" My arms flew out as I gestured at each of them, my hands shaking with my barely controlled anger. "My own mates, who swore to help me get justice for my family's *slaughter*. Or does that not matter to you all now that your problems are solved? Which I helped with, by the way, because your problems fucking matter to me."

We'd destroyed Jeoffrey, which was really a two-for-one special to eliminate Andrei's and Drake's problems. Even Lincoln's problems didn't seem to haunt him the same way anymore, not now that he was making peace with Drake and his childhood trauma within this castle.

I was the only one who needed help now, and they didn't seem to want to give it to me when I needed it most. Pain lanced through my chest, and I fought back the sting of tears that threatened my eyes. That thought hurt more than I cared to admit because they had become my family now. My mates. My best friends. My everything. If they weren't going to help me, then I was right back to being the woman I was when I came to DIA. The woman who was alone against the world.

Drake reached out to grab my hand, but I yanked it away before he could touch it, snarling at him, "Don't."

I knew any of their touches would soften me, and I wouldn't be coerced into backing down.

A raging storm of voices churned in my head, but an overwhelming avalanche of pain, sorrow, and rage filled me. My heart beat loudly in my ears, the blood whooshing as my heart rate rose beat after beat with each of my labored breaths. I felt the bloodhaze coming over me, my emotions reaching dangerous heights.

"Just give yourself some time to think it over," Andrei pleaded, his eyes full of sadness. "Could you kill all the slayers, Alina? What if the slayers are backing House Devaroux entirely? Have you even considered that?"

Before I could answer, Drake was on his feet, backing me up against the wall as I fought to keep distance between us. He eliminated what little space I managed with a few large strides. My chest heaved with anger, brushing against his as he stared down at me. I tried to look away from him, hating the way he peered into my soul, but his hand darted up to grab my chin and anchor it in place.

His voice dropped to a low rumble as he asked, "Do you know what outcome will help you feel at peace, *Comoroă?* Would killing Jade and her family suffice? Because if you don't know, making a plan right now to face them is worthless."

My heart stuttered at the question.

Would killing Jade and her family suffice?

My knees shook as my brain conjured the image of her lying lifelessly on the ground as Skye had. My lips wobbled, and I fought to keep a straight face as tears threatened and my chest squeezed as I considered his challenge.

This was exactly why I needed my fury and nothing else. It was crucial that I stopped thinking with my heart because every single time I thought of where this path would lead me, I pictured having to kill Jade. And I knew I couldn't do it. Even knowing what I do now. Maybe not being able to imagine killing her made me really fucking weak, but she was the last person I had allowed myself to cling to from that life. The one person my soul missed terribly any time I was around Alexandra. Building a new friendship felt impossible with her hanging around in the darkest corners of my heart.

Angry, hot tears rolled down my cheeks despite my best effort to keep them in, only serving to piss me off even more with the knowledge that I was showing my frustration to them this way.

I glared at Drake through my blurry vision, cursing him out in my head for ripping away the fragile rage I'd been clinging to like a life preserver. He'd managed it like it was nothing.

"It doesn't matter," I bit out, my voice thick with emotion. "They must pay for what they've done."

I'd find a way to do it. I *had* to. They all had to pay for what they stole from me.

"Just take a few days to think it through, *please*," Lincoln pleaded, his tone a hell of a lot softer now as he closed the distance to stand at my side.

No.

Suddenly, Andrei was on my other side, effectively blocking me in. My hands clenched into fists as their scents overwhelmed me, leaving me feeling dizzy and off-kilter.

I tried to tip my head up, to look anywhere but at the three of them, but Drake's grip tightened as he growled, "No. You're going to face us right now."

Andrei grabbed my hand, his concern for me bleeding through our bond. "We're worried about you, baby girl. We support you one hundred percent in getting justice for your family, but that doesn't have to happen right this second. It's okay to slow down and just *breathe*."

My tears increased as a sob ripped out of my throat.

That's exactly what I couldn't do. I couldn't slow down and breathe.

"I..." I tried to explain, but my throat was unbearably tight with emotion. I tried to blink away the tears enough to see as I took deep breaths, but it was useless. My heart felt completely shredded and useless in my chest as I admitted, "I can't slow down."

Every muscle in my body tensed, and hot tears continued to stream down my face as memories of my family flooded back. I felt like a fragile house of cards, teetering on the brink of collapse, as emotions I had kept bottled up for so long forced their way out.

"Why, *Comoroă?*" Drake demanded, his touch on my chin softening to brush his thumb along my jaw.

My mouth opened, spilling my truths before I could stop them from flowing out. "Because if I stop going one hundred miles an hour, then all of my demons and suppressed trauma will catch up to me. I can't—" My voice broke, my words faltering as my gaze dropped to his chest. "I'm not strong enough to face it all."

Grief was overwhelming me, choking me like a poisonous fog as it threatened to pull me down to my knees.

I couldn't break now. I needed to keep the lid firmly closed on the box I'd shoved my emotions—*my trauma*—into until everything was handled with the slayers. I had to keep putting one foot in front of the other until my blood oath was fulfilled.

I was so close to it—I couldn't falter at the finish line.

But my resolve was cracking, the jagged splinters of my heart spreading outward until it felt like my body was collapsing in on itself as my head was pulled against a warm, solid chest. Arms of steel wrapped around me, holding me as tightly as I held Serena earlier.

"I can't," I argued weakly to absolutely no one but myself, letting my eyes close as my tears soaked through the soft shirt my cheek was resting against.

Soon, I felt all of them on me, their scents enveloping me in a cloud of comforting energy that only made me fall apart even harder.

Drake's voice was gentle as he pressed a kiss on the top of my head. "You can. We've got you, *Comoroă.*"

All at once, they pushed their love and support through our bonds, entirely splintering me.

Trust us to hold you together when you can't do it yourself, baby girl.

I'll fight every damn demon that haunts you if you can't do it yourself, Spitfire, but you can't keep running from them.

Fuck. Their words left me quaking, and my knees gave out as a flood of trauma and emotions started pouring out. There was nothing I could do to shove it back in. Thoughts and memories bombarded me as I fell apart in their arms.

Being turned into the creature I'd been born and trained to kill.

Killing my best friend with my own fangs and enjoying her blood as I did it.

Losing my entire family and the only home I'd known.

Being barred from my ancestral resting place because of the very venom that changed me into something I had always detested.

Having to drive the sword through my mother's heart as she begged me to end it.

Being forced to go to a school where I was surrounded by everyone who hated me and what I represented as a Van Helsing.

Fighting tooth and nail to not give up on my blood oath while having to accept that I was fated to be with the very people I thought I was supposed to hate.

Those thoughts, emotions, and memories were just the tip of the iceberg, but my fist balled into Drake's shirt as I instinctively fought to push it all back. It was too much.

Too much pain.

Too much suffering.

Too much loss.

It's not weak to open up your wounds, Alina. It takes a hell of a lot of courage to stop pretending like everything's okay and face it, even when it makes your knees tremble and your heart hurt. Even when you feel like it's going to swallow you whole.

A cry of anguish tore from my throat as I finally admitted to myself that I wasn't okay.

I wanted my family back, and there was nothing that could ever make that happen—not even completing my blood oath.

I would never hear the warmth of my parents' voices as they told me how much they loved me and how proud they were of me.

I would never have coffee with my grandmother on our porch as the sun rose, and she reminded me to never dim my shine because the sun never did.

I would never sit at our obscenely large dining room table for the mandatory family dinner we had each week, wishing it would just be over so I could go hang out with my friends.

What I wouldn't fucking give to be sitting at that table with all of them again. I'd taken it all for granted, and now I was left with just the memories, desperately longing to go back in time and let them all know one more time how much I loved them. That even being separated from them in death couldn't stop my love for them.

I wasn't sure how long the emotions poured out of me, but my mates held me tightly for every damn second of it. I sobbed until my throat was raw, and my eyes felt glued shut from how swollen they were.

My parents raised me to believe in myself, my instincts, and, first and foremost, my heart. With the strict law and responsibilities we held as slayers, that last one never made the cut for me, but my mates and friends were finally reminding me of how important it was.

Maybe this was how I needed to honor their memories. Accepting that love wasn't a weakness but our biggest strength.

CHAPTER FOURTEEN
DRAKE

I didn't think it was possible for Alina Van Helsing to own my heart more than she already did. However, as I stared down at her as she slept peacefully, her face still puffy from her last round of crying, I knew her hold on my heart had only increased.

The way she'd finally torn down the last walls around her heart, baring every broken piece of herself to us, was nothing short of breathtaking. Seeing a woman as strong-willed as her finally admit that she wasn't okay... It was truly hard to put into words what it meant to me—to all three of us—that she trusted us enough to show us the depths of the hurt she'd hidden away from even herself.

Brushing a small strand of hair, one that puffed into the air with each breath she exhaled, away from her lips, I let my hand linger on her face, cupping her cheek gently.

It's ready for her.

I didn't want to wake her, but we told her we would take care of her and be here for her, that she could trust us enough to let the pain out. Now that she'd been through cycles of sleeping, grieving, and staring up at the ceiling completely devoid of her normal energy, it was up to us to ensure her needs were met. We intended on following through with our promises to the highest degree.

Gathering her into my arms, I pressed a kiss to her forehead as she grumbled, her brow furrowing. "It's okay, *Comoroă*. I've got you."

Padding to the bathroom, where Lincoln had drawn a bath filled with her favorite scents for her, we made quick work of undressing her, removing the thong and large t-shirt she preferred to sleep in. She roused as I slowly tipped her feet into the water, her beautiful blue eyes hazy but fixated on my face as I continued to dip her into the bath.

"Mmm," she murmured, her eyes closing as the heat enveloped her.

Now that she'd shown us everything she'd been hiding, the bond between us was wide open. Despite sensing her lingering grief, there was a thread of contentment present that I hadn't felt before the breakdown.

Lincoln and I shared a small smile after he settled her head on the foam pillow at the edge of the tub. The corner of her lips turned up into the ghost of a smile.

Lincoln's thought to me was instantaneous. ***Did you see that?***

I offered him a brief nod as I pulled the stool up to the side of the tub, squeezing a dollop of the cherry blossom soap Lo had bought Alina right after she'd met her onto a loofah. Lo had explained that it was the scent that matched Alina the best, and I agreed wholeheartedly with my sister.

I did. It was there, even if it was just for a moment.

She was in a daze as I gently washed her, starting from the tips of her toes and working all the way up her neck. Lincoln helped lean her forward so I could get her back, and after rinsing the soap from the skin there, I took a moment to kiss the marks on the back of her neck that forever displayed our bond for the world to see.

After I finished washing her body, I switched to

holding her as Lincoln washed her hair. It was important to us all to help care for her, and ever since that hard talk a few days ago, we'd fallen into an easy alliance, free of snarky remarks and territorial feelings.

We're running low on animal blood. Which of your staff members can I talk to about replenishing it?

After directing Andrei to the right person, I asked, *How's your mother doing? Is there anything else I can do to make her more comfortable here?*

According to Andrei, she was making remarkable progress and flourishing. Through my bond to Alina, I had felt how important the woman was to her, and so I wanted to do everything in my power to assist her.

Andrei's gratitude flowed through our connection as Lincoln began to rinse the conditioner from Alina's hair.

She's thinking of finding a job somewhere within the main city and getting an apartment there. At first, I thought it was too soon, but it's clear to me that this is something she needs so she can feel like she's reclaiming her life.

I instantly thought of a place run by an old friend that would take on the help if I offered him the right person. And Serena, as sweet as she was, *was* the right person.

Do you think she'd like to work at a flower shop? I have a friend named Marcello that I can speak with.

Lincoln stood to grab the fluffy towels Alina loved as I pulled her out of the bath, drenching my own clothes in the process but not caring in the slightest. As he wrapped her in it, I grabbed the smaller one for her hair and began to dry it gently, rubbing the hair between my towel-covered palms.

I think she'd love that. I'll speak with her and let you know.

I hummed to myself quietly, happy to be able to help.

Oh, and Drake... Thank you for everything. You've done more than I could have ever asked of you. I can't put the depth of my appreciation into words—truly.

We're family now, Andrei, and that includes your mother. We look after our own.

He was silent on the other end of our connection, so I turned my attention back to Alina in time to see her eyes flutter open as we put another large t-shirt on her, this one from Andrei's closet. It was adorable, the way she always reacted when one of our scents enveloped her. We'd taken turns with which of our shirts she wore so that even if one of us wasn't with her, she'd still feel our presence.

Her eyes focused on my face, much more aware of her surroundings than she'd seemed in the past few days. "I'd like to sit outside and get some fresh air today."

Lincoln and I paused briefly. The request felt like a very big step forward, and my pride for her radiated out from my chest toward her.

"By the pool, perhaps?" Lincoln asked, dropping to his knees at her feet with a fresh pair of underwear for her.

She stepped into the holes, and he shimmied them up her long legs and beneath the shirt. "That sounds nice," she answered softly after considering it for a moment.

I felt her uncertainty through the bond and the slight discomfort at the thought of relaxing.

Quickly, I grabbed her hand and lifted it to my lips. I skimmed them over each of her knuckles before bringing our joined hands to my side and pulling her out of the bathroom.

Do not feel bad about this, Comoroă. Please put yourself first for the first time in your life. It isn't selfish.

Her response was hesitant and soft. **Okay... I'll try.**

"Do you want one of us to sit with you, or would you like to be alone?" Lincoln asked gently, grabbing her other hand as we made our way through the castle.

Her hand squeezed mine tightly, like she was afraid of us leaving her. The quick second of panic from him through the bond was enough to tell me that she had squeezed his hand as well.

"We love spending every second with you, Spitfire," he quickly reassured her as we approached the door to the private pool deck. "I just don't want to smother you if you want some time alone."

She nodded as I let go of her hand and pushed the door open for her and Lincoln to go through. As she crossed the threshold, she finally let go of Lincoln's hand, turning to face us.

A small ember of her usual determination shone in her eyes, and my heart skipped a beat as she said, "I think I need to be alone right now. I'll let you know if I need anything."

We nodded and watched her from the doorway as she found one of the half-dome-covered chairs. Grabbing a few towels from the stocked side table, she settled into the padded chair and made a little pillow for herself before wrapping herself in a towel and lying down in it, staring up at the sky.

I had to force myself to close the door and give her the privacy she wanted. Lincoln's jaw flexed as he stared at the door, and I knew we were both struggling to leave her, even for just a moment. Hell, the only time Andrei left her side was for his morning tea with his mom. We'd absolutely been hovering around her, but it was time to let her be if that was what she needed.

I brought my hand up to rest on Lincoln's shoulder and gently squeezed.

We can watch her from a room on the next level while we get some work done.

He begrudgingly nodded, and we headed toward the room after stopping at my office and the study he'd taken to do his own work in. Sending a thought to Andrei to let him know where we would be, we quickly settled into the spare office on the third level that had a clear view of the pool.

***

Her sobs felt like slices of a metal blade to my heart, and the edge of the wood desk I gripped cracked beneath my strength as I stared out at her.

"Fuck," I groaned through gritted teeth, finding it hard to even breathe right now.

For over an hour now, the three of us had

desperately fought off the desire to run down there and hold her in our arms.

"I don't know how much longer I can stay in this room," Lincoln spat, pacing the perimeter of the office for the thousandth time. "I either need to go to the training room and work this off, or I need to go fucking grab her. My bloodhaze is starting to win the battle against my mind."

Andrei rested his head against the window, his arms crossed over his chest as he worked his jaw. Still, he seemed a hell of a lot more stable than Lincoln and me right now, but I could feel the pain in his own heart.

I was impressed by his ability to sort through his emotions and rationalize his thoughts before he turned his gaze on both of us. "Go do what you need to do to ensure you don't interrupt her. This is important for her to do alone, and we can't be selfish about our own needs right now." His eyes shifted back outside as his lips tightened at her keening cry.

"My mother told me this morning that as much as we need the people who love us around us when we're in pain, sometimes what we need even more is to prove to ourselves that in our greatest moment of despair, we are not defeated. That we can rise on our own from it and be stronger in our clarity on the other side."

Serena's words hit me on a visceral level, and I paused, taking a moment to process them.

Lincoln came to a halt, seemingly doing the same.

Logically, I knew that there was truth and wisdom in her words, but fucking hell. It hurt so badly to see Alina out there alone as she processed her repressed emotions and trauma.

"This has been a long time coming," Lincoln said as he put his hands in his pockets and walked to stand next to me. "She's only broken down once that I know of since the death of her family. There wasn't even a fraction of the pain I feel from her now."

Andrei nodded before responding, "We did the right thing by taking a gentle stance with her. None of us wanted to see her make a decision about Jade that she would never be able to take back."

The memory of her face crumbling as I asked her if she could kill Jade hit me square in the chest. If her old friend's demise was what she still wanted on the other side of this, I would gladly rip the slayer's heart out and present it on my finest silver platter to Alina. But I wouldn't act until I could feel with the utmost certainty from my mate's soul that it was what she needed to *really* feel at peace.

Without a doubt, we needed to face Jade's family in a diplomatic meeting to discuss the events that led to them usurping the Van Helsings. Ensuring that they weren't hurting any other families was equally important, but what came of that conversation...no one could really guess. We needed to prepare for all outcomes, and my remaining board members were on standby, ready to assemble for a meeting to discuss plans as soon as Alina was ready to command the conversation.

While I was the King of Sanguis, she was the Queen, and the board was hers to command in this mission. I never wanted to stop her from resolving her blood oath—only to ensure that she wouldn't regret the moves she made.

My chest rumbled as I watched her roll to face the inside of the dome, her small frame shaking as she continued to let her emotions out. "So, we wait for her to come to us now."

"That we do," Lincoln whispered.

We may all have our own problems and different ways of handling situations, but for the first time, I truly understood why we had the *Coniuncta* bond.

We all had to become the best versions of ourselves for her.

My mind paused on something I'd previously told Alina, and I knew I needed to include my new brothers in my quickly forming plan. All I could hope for was that it didn't blow up in my face.

CHAPTER FIFTEEN
ALINA

The stars sparkled in the night sky, staring down at me as hard as I stared up at them. I was lost in a stare-off that I wasn't sure anyone would win at this point.

"Hey, Fate," I called out, finding that the stars reminded me of the ever-mysterious concept of some great... *thing* out there that supposedly lined everything up for us in some kind of predestined way. "It's your girl, Alina."

A star twinkled, illuminating brightly for a moment before fading back into the cluster it resided within.

I blinked twice before rubbing my eyes hard. With the level of mental exhaustion I was at, I was sure that I was seeing things.

"Well...that was fucking weird," I breathed out, searching the sky for any more anomalies. After a few seconds of searching intently, my eyes began to water, and I rubbed them before deciding to give them a rest for just a second. "But anyway, I'd really like to know if..." I trailed off, unsure of how exactly to word my jumbled thoughts.

My brows furrowed as I tried again, swallowing the lump of emotion that lodged itself in my throat as my eyes traveled slowly over the night sky. "I want to know if this pain in my heart will ever go away. Is that a part of my fate?" My voice cracked as I asked the second question, and if I hadn't already cried out every ounce of water in my body, I knew tears would have come. As it was, I was fresh out.

Up for a chat now?

Dev's voice was softer than I'd ever heard it in the time since she barreled into my life and mind. I knew I owed her an apology for how I'd treated her recently, and since I was already spending time making peace with my past, this felt like as good a time as ever.

I flopped onto my back, stretching the cramps out of my arms and legs from being curled up on my side for the majority of the day. My eyes stayed glued to the stars, though, refusing to yield to them in our silent battle.

Yes. I'm sorry, Dev. I've been unfairly harsh with you recently, and you didn't deserve that. I wasn't ready to hear what you were telling me, but that's no excuse for how I treated you when all you wanted was to help me.

The distance in our bond began to close with my apology, and I swear I felt her energy a bit closer to my heart now, making my stomach flutter with joy.

I accept your apology. Thank you.

I let out a heavy sigh. *I've missed you. I know we haven't been connected for long, but it felt wrong to have that space between us.*

Without a doubt, this won't be the only time in our long life that we will disagree, Alina. However, my hope is that you know that even in those moments, I'm always on your team, even if it doesn't feel that way.

My hand came up to rest over my heart, as if I could hold her hand through it.

I know, Dev. I feel that in the very depths of my soul. I promise to listen to you instead of shutting you out from now on.

Silence filled my mind for a long time before she finally asked, **Will you allow me to answer the question you asked Fate?**

If Fate wasn't going to answer me itself, I supposed Dev, who seemed to be an expert on it, was the next best option.

She must have felt my acceptance before I had a chance to speak it because she carried right along, as if she knew this was exactly what I needed to hear.

This pain you feel won't go away completely, and I think you know that. That bit of knowledge was why you were so terrified to allow yourself to feel the extent of it. There will be days the pain will knock you on your ass when you least expect it.

Is there a 'but' coming, or maybe just a little bit of a happy part of this, by chance?

In my current state, I desperately needed something positive to cling to, like a life raft.

Ever the impatient little soul bond, you are— but yes. Although, the pain won't go away completely, it will morph until it becomes a part of who you are, and I mean that in the best way. You will understand yourself on a deeper level, and on those days that the grief does come up and feels suffocating, you will know how to cope with it. You'll know that you have people around you to hold you together while you break, no matter how many times it happens. You will

know that you *can* survive it. So, no, it won't go away, but you will learn how to live with it. For every day that comes after this one, you will be able to put one foot in front of the other, even if someone else who loves you needs to help you move them.

Her words hit me deeply, and I found that I couldn't respond, lost in my mind as I processed them. I let my mind sit with the wisdom of her words and accept them at its own pace, knowing that owning emotional pain wasn't a strong trait of mine.

Dev left me alone to process, and when I finally came out of my pondering state, I felt the relief of less weight pushing down on my chest. My breathing came a little easier, and the idea of leaving my little nest didn't feel quite as unbearable.

One step at a time.

And never alone in your steps.

I took a deep breath. The air stretching my lungs was so immense that this one breath felt like the first one I'd really taken in days. I sucked in just a little more, filling my lungs until they actually hurt. I held my breath for a moment, willing myself to remember this talk with Dev—this moment that felt like a new cornerstone in the foundation of my life.

Tingles spread through my body as I slowly and purposefully let the breath out through slightly parted lips before sitting up. I caught movement out of the corner of my eye. Three figures stood on the level above my room, likely watching over me all day as I fought to keep my head above the wave of grief that had threatened to pull me under.

They tried to move before I caught them, but the more I thought about it, the more I realized there was no doubt my three mates had definitely been keeping an eye on me while still giving me the privacy I needed throughout the day.

My heart yearned to be with them, so I sent out a thought to each of them, telling them I was ready to talk. I asked them to meet me in my bedroom, and as my stomach grumbled, I added that I'd like them to bring a few bags of blood along with them. Despite vaguely remembering each of my mates feeding me the blood I needed to simply survive at some point over the past several days, I knew I needed more. No more surviving on the fringes—it was time to face life head-on.

The relief that flowed to me through our bond was palpable, and I knew with their speed that they would be in the bedroom long before me. Still, I took my time, walking slowly as I soaked in all of the things that reminded me that I needed to keep going. I knew they would wait forever if that's what I needed, so I didn't feel bad about the extra fifteen minutes I took to get to them. Not when I was still processing my new truths.

My vulnerabilities didn't make me weak.

It was okay to not be okay and to ask for help.

The bad days wouldn't always win.

Baring your heart to those you loved made you incredibly brave.

It was okay to listen to your heart first.

As I walked up the steps to the second floor and rounded the corner to my room, I pulled to a stop, taking in the black and red rose petals littering the floor of the hallway that led into my room.

Okay, all three of them are my favorites—I've *officially* decided.

Dev's words made me laugh through the tears that my body had somehow suddenly found the water to produce.

They're my favorites too.

I took the last few steps to my room and stood quietly in the doorway as I took in what they'd done. The rose petals were everywhere, but my eyes caught on how they were shaped into a heart in front of where the three of them stood. Each wore a full black suit, and their handsome faces were illuminated by *hundreds* of candles that were spread throughout the room.

My breath caught in my throat as a tear rolled down my cheek.

Damn it, I didn't want to cry anymore, but this was so fucking sweet.

Drake stepped forward and offered me a hesitant smile, looking somewhat nervous for the first time since I met him. "I know grand gestures aren't your thing from my...previous attempts while you were at DIA, but we wanted to make you feel special and surrounded by love today. The same as we will every day as we move forward together. That's our joint promise to you, *Comoroă.*"

Be still my heart.

A small snort escaped me at the memory of the flower monstrosity that I found outside of my dorm when I was still hellbent on thinking Drake was the villain in my story. My hands flew up to stifle my laugh and eventually brush my tears away.

Lincoln stepped forward, spearing his fingers through his hair as he smirked at me with an easy, lopsided grin. "Those better be happy tears, Princess. Because if they aren't, it's time for me to give up this charade of civility and start laying heads at your feet instead of flowers."

I couldn't hold back my laughter this time, grinning from ear to ear at his words. My laughter stilled on my lips as Andrei stepped forward to join them, all three of them only a few feet away from me now.

"We know that we haven't always made it the easiest to picture a life with all of us in it," he started, and I couldn't help but smile and shake my head. Understatement of the century.

Each of them exchanged looks and chuckled along with me, and damn, it felt good. I needed this. I needed *them*—always.

When we finally stopped laughing, Andrei continued, "But we want you to know that we don't merely accept each other as fixtures in your life anymore. We welcome one another because we've come to see how much you need each of us, and we realized we need each other in our own ways too."

My eyes flicked across each of their faces at his quiet admission. Could I truly hope that his words were the truth?

All at once, their bonds opened to me. My knees wobbled at the outpouring of love and truth I felt from them as they each dropped to one knee.

My mouth fell open as Drake reached into his pocket and pulled out a dark-red velvet box.

Was he—no, he couldn't be. They wouldn't— would they? My mind spun through the possibilities, never once daring to believe what I thought was happening actually was.

My heart hammered in my chest as he opened the box, revealing the most stunning ring I'd ever laid eyes on.

All three of them had their eyes locked on my face as I brushed away the damn tears that refused to stop pouring.

Drake's lips parted, giving me the most stunning smile I'd ever seen, completely wrecking my thin control over my emotions. "Fate may have chosen us for each other, but we wanted to know if you would do the honor of choosing us for the rest of your life?"

A sob ripped from my throat as I full-on ugly-cried, holding my hands over my mouth to attempt to stifle the sound of my gasping breaths.

"We promise to cherish you for forever and a day," Andrei offered quietly, his voice soft and sincere as he reminded me of our conversation in the bathroom when he asked what I would say if he wanted longer than forever.

Somehow, my tears only increased at his promise. It was Lincoln who made my heart feel like it was about to jump out of my chest and onto the heart-shaped flowers in front of their knees as he asked, "Will you marry us, Alina Van Helsing?"

My body moved forward of its own accord, stepping toward them and falling to my knees right in front of them. The motion fully ruined the heart of roses, but I didn't give a fuck. I tried to pull them all to me, struggling to hug all of them at once as my chest heaved with my sobs.

They understood what I needed, just as they always had, and surrounded me with their arms as I let my love for them explode through our bond.

I even heard a few sniffles that weren't my own as I forced my words out.

"You didn't need to do all of this just to ensure I felt loved." I took a second to take a few quick, deep breaths, hiccuping with my effort, before I continued, "I know I was...out of it the past few days, but the one constant I had through it was you all. The way you bathed me, fed me, and held me."

I finally got the courage to pull back from the chest I was buried in, and I took a moment to look at each of them, shocked to see that they had tears misting their eyes as well.

I really meant that much to them. We already

knew that we were all fated and going to spend our lives together, yet they'd gone above and beyond in their desires to make me happy and to claim me.

Fuck. Never in my wildest dreams did I think that we'd all end up here.

"The way you love me is the greatest gift I've ever been given," I said solemnly, meaning the words to the very depths of my being. "You've loved me even when I haven't loved myself, and all I can hope is that I can return a fraction of that love to each of you. I promise that my new lifelong mission will be to make you each feel as loved as you make me feel."

Lincoln grabbed my hip, pulling me close enough to smother my lips with his, his tongue sweeping into my mouth instantly. I opened for him, welcoming his touch as my core ignited with desire.

A throat cleared, and we parted as Drake pinned me with a bemused and affectionate look. "So, is that a yes to being our wife?"

I let out a laugh that shook my body as I nodded and yelled, "It's a hell yes!"

Drake's eyes went black before he grabbed me, melding our chests together as he feasted on my lips, nipping and licking at them.

I love you, Precious.

I gasped, but he swallowed the sound with his mouth. He'd willingly let his monster out to speak to me, too, knowing how much it meant to me to know all of him.

I love you too.

He slowly pulled himself away from me as a new pair of hands pulled me in a different direction. Andrei's hand found my face, cupping my cheek gently as our foreheads fell forward to meet. For a quiet moment, we simply breathed each other in.

"Forever," he murmured, his breath fanning over my lips.

"Forever and a day," I whispered back before tilting my head up to press my lips against his.

My heart soared in my chest, and as my mind thought of my parents and how I wished they could be here to see me find the same deep love that they'd shared, I found that the thought didn't hurt in the same way it would have a few days ago.

Somehow, I knew they were smiling down on all of us, blessing us with their approval all the way from my ancestral resting place.

What I also knew was that I was exactly where I was meant to be, surrounded by the people who made my heart sing.

CHAPTER SIXTEEN

ALINA

s Drake slid the beyond-gorgeous ring onto my finger, my mouth popped open. From a distance, I thought it was beautiful. But up close? Absolutely breathtaking.

A dark grey gem with black lines running through it like small bolts of dark lightning met my hungry gaze. It was diamond-shaped and set in the center of a cluster of diamonds. My breath caught in my chest as I stared at the beautiful work of art resting on my finger. With awe evident in my voice, I asked, "What kind of stone is this? I've never seen something so unique, so perfect."

Honestly, I never allowed myself the opportunity to consider the type of ring I wanted. Hell—I'd been dead set on not getting married for the majority of my life, knowing I'd be forced into an arranged marriage. Yet somehow, they'd picked out something absolutely perfect for me.

I let out a small breath, shaking my head at my own thoughts. I don't even know why that shocked me. Sometimes it felt like these men knew me better than I knew myself.

"It's a black rutilated quartz," Drake murmured, his voice dripping with a seductive energy that pulled my eyes from the ring to him.

My tongue darted out to wet my lips at the sight of his tented pants. I sucked my bottom lip into my mouth, biting down on it. Was it hot in here, or was it just my mate? My future *husband*.

"Doesn't she look fucking stunning with our ring on her finger, brothers?" he purred as he stalked around to my back.

A shiver ran through me.

I wasn't sure what was more attractive, the way he said those words or the fact that he called them brothers. Either way, I was a mess of need in an instant. The exhaustion and limpness I'd felt in my body a few hours ago were nowhere to be found—I was completely replenished with the energy these men fed my soul.

"Delicious," Lincoln agreed, coming to my right side as Andrei approached the other.

I sucked my bottom lip between my teeth as Andrei added, "Good enough to eat if you ask me."

Fucking hell, the way these men could turn me on should be illegal.

Fingers pulled my hair away from my neck, moving it over my shoulder until it cascaded down my back, before they returned to gently caress my now exposed skin. A shiver ran through me at the feel of the light touch, and my clit pulsed with desire.

My breathing turned shallow as I tilted my head to the side to give them further access. It earned me a rumble of approval that I could feel from Drake's hard chest pressed in tightly against my back. Softly, he growled, "I think she'd look even more delectable in nothing but our ring."

My eyebrows knit together at his words. I didn't have any other jewelry on.

But as Lincoln and Andrei moved as one, pulling the long shirt from my body as Drake ripped my thong in half, it made sense.

They wanted me naked and exposed, with only the ring that claimed me as theirs on my body—and I fucking loved it.

My thighs felt slick with my arousal as I rubbed them together, and the anticipation of what they would do next made my skin feel like it was on fire.

"We've marked your skin with the bond mark," Lincoln murmured, running his hand up the outside of my leg and slowly up to my hip.

Andrei grabbed my left hand and lifted it to kiss before adding, "We've marked your hand with old traditions to claim you."

Drake's hand slowly trailed down my spine, making the hair on my arms stand on end with the feather-light, yet electric touch.

"All that's left is to mark the inside of your body as ours. It's been far too long since you've had our cum inside of you, *Comoroă*."

I couldn't agree more, and the thought of having them all together... There wasn't anything I wanted more right now.

My breathy voice was airy and seductive as I asked, "Who's going to remedy that little problem for me?"

Before I could blink, Lincoln was throwing me over his shoulder and racing toward Drake's room. He tossed me on the bed, and I fought a giggle as I bounced.

Instead, my lips tugged into a smirk as I pushed

up onto my elbows, kicking my feet, which hung slightly off the edge of the bed.

"Why was I moved here?" I asked, my voice full of faux innocence. My eyes traveled to where I knew the cuffs were tucked away in the corners of the bed frame. I let my voice drop an octave lower as I looked back up to the three of them standing in front of me and purred, "Do you anticipate me being a bad girl?"

Andrei let out a groan, almost like he was in pain, as he brought his fist up to his mouth, biting down on his knuckles. His eyes rolled back slightly as I spread my legs, resting my heels on the edge of the bed and exposing myself to them.

I knew he would give me everything I needed the second I asked for it.

A flurry of excitement rolled through me as I saw Lincoln's eyes narrow on me, his hands curling into fists at his side. It was too much fun pushing my broody professor to accept that he wasn't in control, but I ached for the fight for it. I would always ache for it, too.

"What's wrong, Linc?" I teased, my eyes narrowing back at him in challenge. "Cat got your tongue?"

His body vibrated with barely restrained control for a few seconds before he snapped, but I was ready. As he lunged for me, I jumped up and darted to the side. His body hit the mattress as I prowled behind Drake, who stared at us with bemused interest, arms folded across his chest.

"Too slow," I chirped in a sing-song voice, running my fingers along Drake's back as I shot Andrei a wink.

"Get over here right now, Princess," Lincoln growled, standing to his full height as he pulled off his suit jacket.

I sashayed over to Andrei and pressed up onto my tiptoes, offering Lincoln a view of my ass with the movement. As soon as our lips met, Andrei's hands were all over me, caressing my back all the way down to my ass before grabbing a handful.

His erection pressed against my abdomen, and I pulled back enough to look at his sparkling green eyes before demanding, "Strip for me."

As he began to do as I requested, I glanced over my shoulder to find Lincoln patiently rolling up the sleeves of his black dress shirt. His gaze was hot and heavy on me, running up and down the length of my body.

"I'm giving you three seconds, Princess," he warned, and my clit pulsed with his words.

I let out an indignant laugh, ignoring him and

returning my gaze to Andrei's tanned, rippling muscles that were revealed to me as he unbuttoned his shirt. I licked my lips instinctively and smirked at him as Lincoln began to countdown.

"Three."

Are you going to get a head start? Andrei asked, smirking back at me as he let the black material fall off his shoulders to pool on the floor behind him.

"Two."

No, but you might want to jump out of the way unless you want to be in a cuddle puddle on the floor with him.

"One."

I darted away, but I found myself running straight into Drake's hard chest as his hands wrapped tightly around my arms, effectively trapping me. The sudden stop knocked some of the air from my lungs, and my brain short-circuited from being so suddenly cut off from my little game with Lincoln.

All the bratty energy trickled out of me as I tipped my head back, finding hooded eyes staring back down at me. "I can smell your arousal, *Comoroă*. I've let you have your fun, but do you remember what I said the first time you were in this room with me?"

My brain struggled to recall as I turned into a puddle at the way he silently took control of me, like it was as easy as breathing. The way my body submitted to him with such ease would forever be a conundrum to me.

"I...I don't," I breathed out, blinking rapidly as I continued to rack my brain.

One of his hands moved to grab my chin as he raised a single eyebrow. My lips parted in desire at the stern tone he took with me as he said, "Then let me refresh your memory. In here, I'm in control. You don't get to come until I let you, and I will fuck you wherever I want, whenever I want, and in front of whoever I want."

His eyes flicked up at the end of his statement to the two men I felt closing in behind me.

As he let go of my chin, his head jerked toward the massive bed. "Now be a good girl and get back on the bed."

The way I wanted to give in to him was strange, but then it was like my body suddenly remembered Andrei and Lincoln were here, and it fought to switch into the roles I took with each of them. I was on overload because I couldn't possibly be all three versions of myself at the same time.

So which side of me would win right now?

What part of me did I *want* to come out?

Relax, baby girl. I can feel anxiety creeping up within you. At the end of the day, you will always be in control of these moments, no matter what any of us say. We worship the ground you walk on. Just do what feels right, and we will follow your lead.

Andrei's words were like a balm to my frazzled brain, and the tension that I hadn't recognized coiling in my chest faded away.

I wanted them to make me feel good, and I knew they would if I let them. I didn't need to force any one side of me out to play just to please one of them —I simply needed to *be*.

I batted my eyes up at Drake as I stuck my bottom lip out to pout. "I will, but only if you promise not to make me wait long to come. I need it."

The corner of his lip tilted up as he gave me a small nod and said, "Your wish is my command. But just remember that you asked me to not hold back."

I wasn't sure exactly what I was asking for with my stipulation—considering these men loved to torture me by withholding my orgasms, I just hoped it would be less of that. But as Drake's hands found my hips and my vision blurred as he moved me to the edge of the bed, I knew it wouldn't be that simple.

So quickly, it felt instant—he and Lincoln pushed me on the bed, bent at the waist, with my ankles cuffed to the bottom of the frame and my wrists cuffed to the sides. My chest was pressed flat against the mattress, and my legs were spread wide for them.

The sound of drawers creaking open pulled my attention, and I attempted to lift my head enough to see what was going on behind me, but I couldn't. I shifted around, not giving up on my pursuit, but when a loud buzzing sound met my ears, I froze.

What the hell?

I let out a yelp of surprise as my ass jerked to the side in shock. Something vibrating was pressed against my clit at the same time a toy was pushed into my pussy. My body was on overdrive, desperately trying to catch up to the intensity shooting through me.

"Holy shit," I panted, my breaths coming out short and labored. "It's too much."

On instinct, I tried to pull my legs closed to get away from whatever the hell was on my clit. But as I tried to pull away from the intense pleasure, my face fell forward to press into the soft bedspread. A moan ripping out of me, and I could feel the tremors of an orgasm beginning to build within me.

Whoever controlled the toy within me pulled it in and out over and over again, methodically working me up as the intensity of the vibration on my clit increased. Tears gathered in my eyes, and at the moment, I honestly couldn't tell if it was from pleasure or pain. Whatever the source of the tears, it was one of the most intense experiences I've ever had.

I was completely lost to the sensations in my body, and my hips began to try to rock, finding my pace. A hand swatted my ass, adding to the burning sensation already soaring beneath my skin.

"You wanted to come, Princess," Lincoln grumbled.

"So come for us," Drake added.

A cry slipped out of me as I felt my body reaching for it, shaking in my quest. My legs trembled from the pressure building to a fever pitch within me.

"That's right, baby girl," I heard Andrei coo as a hand trailed down my back. "Let go."

Pressure built within me as the toy was pulled from my pussy. The vibrations on my clit remained, as intense as ever, and I exploded, feeling the gush of my orgasm trailing down my legs.

I didn't have a moment to think about my reaction as my body sagged in relief, the torturous pleasure finally being removed from my clit.

Drake had taken my words seriously, of fucking course.

"So," the devil himself drawled, "now that we've given you what you wanted, it's time to give us what we want."

I was too busy panting and trying to catch my breath to even attempt asking what that was. Thankfully, Lincoln filled in the blanks, and my eyes went wide at the demand.

"Beg for our cocks, Princess. You won't be able to touch a single inch of us with any part of your body until you do."

CHAPTER SEVENTEEN
LINCOLN

I was absolutely testing my own limits with the command, but fucking hell. I wanted her to beg for me more than I needed blood to survive.

I wanted her to beg for me to fill her pretty little pussy up with my cum.

I wanted her body shaking in need of what I could give her.

I don't know how long I can wait to sink into her, Andrei admitted from my side as we stood behind her, staring at her glistening pussy. **You're asking a hell of a lot right now.**

My eyes narrowed to slits as I shoved my wrist, adorned with his dumb-ass friendship bracelet, in his face. *If I can wear this all the damn time, you can hold your dick in your hand while we wait for her to give in to us.*

A bemused smirk tugged at his lips. **Fine, but let's drive her crazy so she gives in quickly.**

I grunted in agreement just as my little princess began to whine, her bratty side rearing its head. "That is so not fair! I know you all want to fuck me as badly as I want it. Can't we all just agree to give into our needs?"

She tugged at the restraints, the metal chains rattling against the heavy wood frame of the bed. My eyes tracked her perky ass, jiggling with the movement, and my cock twitched in my pants, desperate to sink into her wet heat.

Drake began to strip his shirt off as his gaze swung to me. **I normally take control, but I'll concede it to you if you think you can tame her.**

A huff of laughter puffed over my lips as I approached her. *I know what I'm doing.*

Normally, I employed a harsher, more physical show of force to get her to submit, but tonight I had another idea. There was a small shift in her demeanor over the past few days, and something new had awoken in me when I saw it here tonight.

I softened my tone as I ran a finger down her spine. "Princess, don't you want our cocks?"

The subtle jerk of her head told me she was shocked by my soft tone, but she quickly cooed back, "Yes. I do."

Trailing my touch down to her pussy, I gently sank a finger into her, loving the way her head flipped to face me. Her eyes widened with an adorable pleading look that made my cock jump.

Her hips rolled back as I began to pump it in and out of her, knowing that just having the one finger working her would drive her fucking crazy.

As her lips parted and her pupils dilated, I knew I fucking had her with this new method. Maybe we didn't always need to be so rough with each other in our fight for control, after all.

"Don't you want to be my good little Princess?" I questioned, using my free hand to brush strands of her silver locks out of her face. "I want to give you what you need, but you've got to give me this."

A heavy sigh puffed over her lips, and a small scowl knitted her brow. All I did in response was curl my finger, hitting her favorite little spot. Her forehead smoothed as a breathy moan slipped out of her.

After her lashes fluttered a few times, her beautiful eyes bore into my soul as she asked so fucking nicely, "Please, Linc?"

Fucking hell. I thought nothing could ever compare to the way she fought me before relenting, but this... Hell, it was enough to force me to take a deep breath and try not to blow my load in my pants like a teenager.

She was almost there, but not quite, and I wasn't going to give in until she properly submitted to my demands. Deciding she deserved a small reward for working in the right direction, I added a second finger, enjoying the way her back arched as much as it could in her position. She let out a small cry of need.

"That was so close, Princess, but you need to say everything I requested."

Her bottom lip stuck out in a pout, still fighting me. But it was clear that she was enjoying this change of pace as well, her pussy tightening around my fingers.

She huffed before relenting. "Please fuck my pussy with your cock, *Sir*."

I couldn't help but smirk at that attitude of hers, which I loved so much, peeking through. Rolling my thumb over her clit and making her gasp, I chided, "Without the attitude and a lot more fucking enthusiasm, Princess."

As I heard rustling and clanking sounds behind

me, I glanced over my shoulder to find Andrei and Drake butt-fucking-naked, stroking their cocks as they watched. That was a change to adjust to, but the reminder of their involvement gave me an idea.

Come closer. Tease her ass with just the tip of your cock, I sent to Andrei. *I know you went there with her and know how to handle her gently.*

He licked his lips and nodded as he stepped forward. I switched my focus back to Alina as she stared at me, tight-lipped and waiting for my next move.

Removing my fingers from her pussy, I dragged her wetness up to her asshole, coating her entrance with her own arousal. I smirked, watching her eyes widen as I stretched my hands over her ass cheeks and spread them for Andrei as he approached.

As his tip brushed against her, I glanced down at her. "I'm allowing this touch because it seems that you might need a reminder of how you screamed with Andrei's cock buried in your ass the other night."

The vein in her neck strained and pounded faster. My nostrils flared at the renewed scent of her arousal flooding the air.

As she swallowed hard, I pressed on. "I stood

outside the fucking door listening to the way you moaned, Princess, stroking my cock as I pictured it."

I knew for a fact that she loved being watched, and I'd been holding onto that tidbit of information for a perfect moment like this.

A moan slipped from her lips as her eyes fluttered closed.

"Look at me, Princess," I demanded sharply, and I was quickly rewarded with her lust-dazed eyes locking with mine. "Tell me, and you can have it."

This time, when her lips parted to speak, I knew her words were going to be everything I wanted. Her body was putty under us—there was no tautness in her restraints any longer. The lust pouring through our bond was also at an all-time high.

"Please, I need your cocks," she begged, a whine in her voice that felt so fucking genuine. "I need them all so fucking bad."

I'm done waiting now, Drake sent to me as he came to her other side. ***Let's get rid of the restraints so we can get her in a better position for us.***

Andrei gave me a questioning look, and I nodded at him as he grabbed his cock and lined it up with her pussy. He sank into her, pulling a deep moan from her as Drake and I freed her arms and legs.

I couldn't deny that the sound of her moans as

their skin slapped together turned me the fuck on. I never thought watching or listening to her with another guy could do anything to me other than send me into a haze of jealous rage, but I'd been proven wrong the night I went to her room and heard them together. I'd come so fucking hard in my hand as I listened to them finish.

Andrei's grunts joined Alina's mewling as he pounded in and out of her but the moment he noticed that she was free of her bindings, a wicked smile crossed his lips as he pulled out and slapped her ass.

She let out a yelp of surprise, but we didn't leave her waiting for long.

Andrei headed for where Drake told us his supplies were as we prowled toward her.

As I claimed the spot next to her, lying on my back, she climbed over me, grabbing my cock and sinking down onto me with a greedy smile on her face. I pulled her chest down to press against mine and buried my hand in the hair at the base of her neck as I slowly rocked my hips up into her.

"You feel so fucking good, Princess," I whispered, and was instantly rewarded with the walls of her pussy tightening around my cock.

The bed dipped with Drake's weight, and I

lightly yanked her hair, turning her face toward him, her mouth opening with a small hiss. Her pussy clenched around me with the move, and I knew it didn't actually hurt her.

"Open wide, *Comoroă*," Drake instructed with a chuckle, his cock in hand. "You know damn well I'm not going to fit in as is."

She greedily opened for him as he pushed forward, and I used my hand in her hair to force her to take him in deeper, controlling the pace for both of them. I was initially worried that it might be awkward to figure out how to share her, but I was quickly learning that sharing her opened me up to so many new options with her—ones that I was quickly finding myself a fan of.

Her throat bulged with the girth of him, and I groaned at the sound of her choking slightly on his cock.

"Breathe, Princess," I said, loving the way she instantly did as I taught her, relaxing her jaw enough to take him in further as she breathed through her nose.

Andrei's knees settled on the outside of my legs as I heard the telltale sound of the lid cracking open on a bottle. My free hand found her hip, and I brushed my fingers softly along her skin in a silent show of support. I slowed my pace to give Andrei a moment to coat himself and Alina with the lube, tossing it onto the bed next to me a moment later.

I felt the way she tightened as he began to push, and I wasn't sure she would be able to take us both at the same time.

Drake took over in that moment, taking her hair from me as he tilted her head up to look at him with his cock still buried in her throat. "You're doing so fucking good, *Comoroă*," he praised, pulling back to let her breathe easier. "Relax your body and take both of them in. You were fucking made for us. You can do it."

She did as he said, her vice-like grip on my cock easing, and after a few moments, I felt Andrei's cock rubbing up against my own between the thin barrier separating us.

I tried to keep my grip on her hip soft, but as he fully settled within her, my fingertips dug into her soft flesh. The feeling was fucking mind-blowing, and all I wanted to do was move inside of her, but I knew she needed a moment to adjust.

Dragging my now hair-free hand down, I slipped it between us and rubbed her clit until she moaned around the tip of Drake's cock. His eyes rolled back.

Can I move, Princess?

I think I might die if you don't.

With a chuckle, I tentatively flexed my hips up and back down while Andrei remained still.

You're not going to break me, Sir. Fuck me.

"Our girl wants it all," I drawled to Andrei as I met his gaze behind her.

We found our pace, starting off slow and steady and building when we saw she wasn't in pain. Drake began to fuck her throat, his pace increasing along-side our own until the air was filled with a cacophony of our combined sounds.

"Fucking hell," Andrei groaned, throwing his head back as he thrust into her. The gargled sound of Alina moaning hit me hard.

I couldn't agree with Andrei more. Between seeing her being shared like this and the feeling of the two of us inside of her at once, I knew I wasn't going to last long.

Moving my hand to slide up her throat beneath where Drake's cock fucked into her throat, I held her there and squeezed just how my princess liked.

Dropping my voice to the rumble that always makes her fall apart for me, I growled, "Do you like being filled with all of our cocks, Princess? You're going to be dripping from every fucking hole with our cum like our good little girl."

Her eyes rolled back as a new slickness covered my cock, spurring me to fuck her faster, knowing she was nearing her peak.

"If you want our cum, you're going to have to work for it, Princess," I purred. "Squeeze our cocks like you want us to mark you, and we'll give it to you."

I'm so fucking close, Linc.

Her needy tone turned me feral, and I pounded into her, giving her everything I had.

My balls clenched, and I knew I was seconds away from finishing. I needed my mate to come before me, and I was determined to make it happen.

"Come for us, Princess," I demanded. "Be our good girl."

The moment I felt the bliss of her orgasm washing through our bond, I exploded. Within seconds, I felt Andrei and Drake in the bond following suit, claiming her in the final way we all wanted—our seed inside her as she blissed out.

Our heavy pants and uneven breathing filled the air. And except for Drake pulling out of her mouth, none of us moved.

"Holy fucking shit," she breathed out, craning her neck to look at all of us.

We all echoed various statements of agreement, soaking in the moment.

Best damn orgasm of my life.

As Andrei pulled out of Alina, she collapsed onto me. I wrapped my arms around her, holding her close as I brushed my fingers across her damp skin.

"You're incredible, Alina," I said before pressing a kiss to the top of her head as I watched Drake and Andrei walk to the en suite bathroom.

The sound of the shower running met my ears, and my heart settled as the need to take care of her swelled within me. It was relieving to know that I didn't need to rush to do it myself because they had her too.

"I know," she sassed back with a giggle before propping her chin up on my chest to gaze at me.

Maybe to someone else, feeling pride swell over her agreement would sound arrogant or conceited, but to me, they were two of the best words I'd ever heard. The fact that they came from a woman who admitted to feeling lost and forced into a mold her whole life... Even better.

She was blossoming into a confident and self-assured woman who loved deeply and would do anything for those she claimed as hers.

My heart soared at hearing her own that.

I reached up to brush my thumb across her cheek, loving the way she leaned into my touch and closed her eyes.

Bliss washed through our bond as I whispered, "Don't you ever fucking forget it."

CHAPTER EIGHTEEN
ALINA

My eyes cracked open from what was the most blissful sleep of my life as my bladder screamed at me, insisting I get the hell up to use the bathroom. I attempted to sit up but found myself completely wrapped in a jumble of my mates' limbs, incapable of moving an inch. They had me effectively trapped.

Hair stuck to the back of my neck, the skin damp from the heat of the little nest we'd formed, and I knew a shower was next on the list after relieving myself.

The moment I tried to wiggle free and slide out from beneath them, groans of disapproval sounded, and I let out a soft laugh. "You three haven't let me leave this room in days, other than to go to Drake's room to use *that* bed. As much as I love you all, I need to pee and shower."

The days spent together in a lust and love-filled haze had been amazing for our bonds. For the first time, I truly felt like we were operating as one. Watching them all deepening their own connections to one another had melted my heart into a puddle of goop in my chest, but we couldn't stay here forever. No matter how tempting it was.

"And we can't ignore the reality waiting at our doorstep any longer."

As the haze of excitement from the proposal and the bliss of our many love-making marathons wore off, I felt an intense need to face my final problem overwhelm me. My mind felt sharp and clear for the first time in forever, and as I considered how I wanted to handle the situation with Jade, my heart knew the path it needed to take.

My decision wasn't made in rage or based on what I thought I had to do to fulfill my blood oath any longer. It was based simply on what my heart knew was the right path for me to finally feel peace within my soul. It was time to face the House of Devaroux and all the slayers who backed them.

"One more day," Andrei pleaded, staring up at

me from where he was sprawled across my lower legs.

As I pursed my lips and narrowed my eyes at his puppy-dog eyes, his hands snaked down to grab my foot and began massaging it.

"That's cheating!" I shrieked, attempting to dislodge my foot from his magical hands, which always managed to convince me to do what he wanted.

All I had to say was thank the Fates for rapid healing, because the things these men had done to my body... I couldn't imagine being a human and having to recover from it.

Lincoln began to trail kisses up my arm as Drake cuddled further into my other side, dropping his heavy arm over my waist.

These men—entirely insufferable currently— were completely *mine*.

I let out a groan as my head fell back against my pillow with a heavy thud. "I swear I will pull Dev out to kick all of your asses if you don't let me up to use the bathroom right now!"

Dev scoffed loudly.

A soul weapon is meant to fight in great battles—ones that are spoken of in history books long after the wielder has passed from this

world. Yet you threaten to use me for what? The Great Bathroom Battle of Sanguis?

I rolled my eyes good-naturedly and let out a laugh. She was just jealous that she wasn't able to have orgasms of her own.

Drake let out a heavy groan as he pulled his arm off me and rolled over to give me an opening. "Are you ready for me to call the board together?"

His voice was rough from sleep still, and as I kissed Lincoln as payment to be let out from beneath him, I gave his words some thought.

Were the remaining board members trustworthy enough to have such a meeting with them?

Could I trust them not to fuck up something so important to me?

Andrei peppered the tops of my feet with kisses before rolling off the bed and heading for the bathroom with the promise of seeing me in the shower shortly.

After separating from my grumbly professor, I scooted my ass to sit on the edge of the bed next to Drake, threading our hands together as I made my decision.

We glanced at each other at the same moment, and I gave him a small nod, sure of the path ahead of us now.

"Call the board."

***

An hour later, we found ourselves situated around the conference room table, waiting for one last person to arrive before I launched into my plan. Nerves erupted in my stomach like a swarm of butterflies. I chewed my lip, trying to calm the thoughts of my plan being received poorly by everyone here.

There was a long history of violence between the slayers and vampires, and what I had in mind... Well, it would change everything.

Rolling my shoulders back, I lifted my chin and took a deep breath. I was ready to fight for the future I knew would unite the two factions and end the senseless bloodshed and hatred that existed between them.

I sat at the head of the table—typically reserved for Drake—and as I glanced around at my allies, I knew they would at least be willing to hear me out.

Tania, Heather, and Kiyomi had proven to be loyal through our battle with Jeoffrey. Without a doubt, their loyalty was to Drake, but I hoped to prove to them, and every single vampire and slayer in Sanguis, that I was someone they could have pride in following as well.

The heavy double doors pushed open, and my heart fluttered in my chest as Lo walked in, radiant and glowing as she offered me a full smile. Her heels clacked loudly against the floor as she came to take her seat to my right. With a wink and a nod that boosted my confidence tenfold, she settled in and waited for me to begin.

We had so damn much to catch up on, seeing as she had been with Oleander this entire time. I pushed away the urge to pull her out of the conference room and gush about her bond with her, knowing there would be plenty of time for that soon.

I cleared my throat, scanning my mates' faces on the left side of the table for a moment. Their support and love radiated back to me through our bonds, and I knew now was as good a time as ever to put my plan in motion.

You can fucking do this. You're Alina Van Helsing, Queen of Sanguis. If ever there was someone who could pull this off, it's you. Believe.

My chest burned with pride. The boost of confidence was exactly what I needed.

"Thank you all for coming on such short notice," I started, inclining my head in greeting to each member. "I know there has been chaos, deceit, and, unfortunately, the loss of lives by people we thought of as allies. While they chose their side in the battle, it doesn't take away from the sadness that lingers in my heart with the knowledge that their side fought to take over the board to push back against the slayers and our king."

I took a second to take a deep breath and center my thoughts before I pushed on. "It is no secret that I was once a slayer from the most prominent House. I upheld their laws and traditions to the best of my ability my entire life, until I lost my family in a planned attack. Transitioning into a vampire and enrolling at Dark Imaginarium Academy allowed me to see the flaws that exist on both sides of this lifelong feud. My goal is to mend the burned bridges and establish a joint ruling system."

Lo's head tilted to the side, but she remained silent, seemingly mulling over my words. It was a much better reaction than the spluttering and coughs that came from Heather and Tania. Kiyomi just stared at me with wide eyes, apparently shocked into silence.

I swallowed hard as I prepared to glance at my mates and see their reactions. None of them pushed me to tell them my plans beforehand, so this was a bombshell for them as much as it was for the rest of the board.

"It's about time for some change around here," Lincoln stated, clasping his hands together on the table in front of him. He gazed around at everyone at the table as he continued, "I personally had an awful experience with guards and board members as a child, especially during a very traumatic time in my life. All it did was teach me to not trust my leaders and to think of all those in power as heartless bastards that didn't have their subjects' best interests at heart."

My lips thinned as I recalled his story, and I couldn't help but nod in agreement. So much needed to change. Not just for me but for all within our lands, so that anyone in need, like Lincoln once was, knew they could come to us.

Andrei clapped Lincoln on the back, nodding his agreement before addressing the board. "We all know that I was raised by a heartless bastard who craved power. He raised me to believe that no one could or *would* help my mom or me out of the situation we were in. He taught me that deception and abuse of power were the only tools one needed in life."

His gaze swung to me as a small smile teased the

corners of his lips. "Alina taught me that there's another way to live. One where we trust in our friends, lovers, and allies to have our backs. I couldn't think of a better person to teach that lesson, especially at the scale she's suggesting."

I bit down on my bottom lip to try to ground myself, filled with so much love that it almost hurt as my eyes turned to Drake. His gaze was already on me, and we stared in silence at one another for a few moments.

He was the one I feared hearing feedback from the most. He'd built Sanguis into what it is today, dedicating every single day to trying to make it into a thriving society that all vampires could find a home within. I'd drive Dev through my heart again if he thought my idea was a dig at what he had done with these lands.

Do you truly think it can be done? he asked, tone devoid of judgment. A sense of intense curiosity flowed through our bond.

Yes, I absolutely do.

That's all it took for Dracula, leader of Sanguis and the most feared of our kind, to give me his nod of approval before announcing to the room, "I will do all I can to see this come to fruition."

While his society wasn't built on democracy and

the board didn't operate in that manner, it was still important to me to have the support of everyone in the room. We would need as many strong minds as possible to help us transition to the new world waiting for us on the other side of this fight.

"It won't be easy, Alina," Lo warned, pulling my attention back to the right side of the table and seeing her brows raised as she shook her head. "We're talking about generations of hatred and bloodshed that have shaped this land. It won't happen overnight or without struggle."

My response was instant—feeling certain that this was the way toward a united future. "Nothing easy is ever worth it. I won't stop until these dreams are achieved. I won't allow our future generations to face the same devastating moments we and our predecessors did. There's no need for us to live in fear of one another."

I wasn't sure if it was the conviction with which I said it or something else entirely, but I felt the shift within her before she lifted her head and stood. With her fist over her heart, she announced, "You have my sword, Queen Alina. This is a future that I will fight to the end for."

Kiyomi stood to her feet, crossing her fist to her heart as well. Staring at me, a hard edge of determination met my gaze as she said, "My sword is yours. May we build a future that we can one day leave behind without fear for those who come after us."

My eyes burned with emotion as my throat tightened. All of this support was... Fuck, it was everything. I'd hoped they'd agree to possibly talk about the options. To feel their confidence in what was just presented as an idea without details was more than I dared consider as an outcome.

Heather and Tania stood to their feet at the same time, following suit with fists over their hearts as they bowed their heads briefly to me and to Drake.

"I will serve the crown and our people until the end," Tania declared.

Heather took a deep breath before her hand darted to wipe her eyes. The emotion etched so clearly on her face brought tears to my own eyes, and I fought to not let them fall as she spoke. "There is nothing more I could ask for than the ability to one day say that I helped bring about peace and prosperity to these great lands. I'm honored to be in this room with all of you, and I truly believe we can achieve what might feel impossible right now."

Fucking hell, ever since my long-overdue break- down, it's like I couldn't turn off my tear ducts. I tried, I really did, but I lost the battle with the damn things, and tears poured down my cheeks as I nodded at everyone in the room. I fought to find the words to thank them for their support.

My throat was tight as I swallowed. I took a deep, calming breath before speaking. "Thank you, all of you, for your support. While it might have been me that brought the idea forth, I know that I cannot accomplish this feat alone. It will take the might of all of our hearts and souls to see this through to the end."

I lifted my hands to wipe away the tears, and a warmth entered my heart that I'd never experienced before. It felt like...home.

Mom? Dad?

They'll always be watching over you. Continue to make them proud, Alina.

CHAPTER NINETEEN
ALINA

Feeling my parents' warmth gave me the boost I needed to suck in the tears and forge on. I had felt the peace in my soul when I'd first thought of my plans, but to feel their presence and support was what would get me through the hard times.

"It's great that we want peace and to find a new way to live in unity," I said, folding my hands in my lap. "But the real question is how we get there, right?" Heads bobbed around the table for a moment before I continued, "I would like to push for a diplomatic meeting tomorrow with the ruling slayer House. The hope is to discuss new terms for a peace treaty."

Andrei seemed to choke on his spit, and he had

to take a few seconds to clear his throat and gather himself before asking, "The House of Devaroux? You want to be *diplomatic* with them?"

If he had asked me the same question a week ago, I would have laughed in his face like a maniac. The mere thought of my vengeance being ripped away from me—I probably would have whipped Dev out. But now... It wasn't about vengeance. It was about justice.

"Yes," I responded, not allowing even the slightest bit of venom to drip into my tone. I wanted to lead by example, and that started now—no matter how fucking hard it was going to be. "I want to speak to them about the night of my family's murder before deciding what to do with them."

My gaze swung to Drake as I began to lay down the necessities required for my plan to work. "Do we have access to someone from Victoria's bloodline who would be willing to help us? If I remember correctly, their line can pick up on the moods of those around them without even tasting a drop of their blood. Could they then, in turn, sense if someone was lying because of their change in mood?"

Drake's head inclined as his brow furrowed. He pondered the question for a moment before responding, "We would need the strongest of their line to discern something that specific, and unfortunately, Priska has made it clear to everyone in Sanguis that she adamantly wishes to be left out of political battles."

Pulling my lip between my teeth, I nibbled on it as I tried to think of how I might be able to convince her to help us in such a short amount of time.

Shit. That was a vital part of my plan. We had to find a—

My thoughts were cut off when Lo pushed to her feet. She tilted her head down at me, as serious a look on her face as I've ever seen, and said, "I will head to her home and plead our case. I have had an outstanding favor to collect from her that I have been waiting for the perfect moment to use."

I could fucking kiss her right on the mouth.

"Thank you," I said, relief washing through me like a wave as I offered her a nod. Without another word, she turned to leave at once.

I waited until the doors closed behind her to move on to the next part of the plan. "We will use Priska's abilities to determine whether or not they were involved in any way with the deaths of my family. It didn't sit right in my heart to simply take Jeoffrey and a seedy witch's words at face value. I want to be certain, and if the House Devaroux is found guilty, I want them to go on trial—the very first one that will be judged by slayers and vampires alike."

"You're certainly not holding any punches with your vision of the future," Drake murmured, but I heard the pride in his tone. "What would you have us do if they are found guilty and they choose to fight us rather than accept their punishment?"

I heaved a deep breath, positive that the Devaroux slayers would absolutely fight us if that were the case. This was where things could get dicey, but I trusted the judgment of those around me.

"If you are unable to immobilize them and your life is endangered—kill them," I stated, my blood boiling at the thought. I wouldn't allow anyone else to be killed by them just because I decided to appease my desire for justice with mercy. I took a second to look each of them in the eye before I stated, "Your lives come first. Do not hesitate, even if excessive force is needed. Do you understand me? We are *all* coming home after this."

After receiving nods of confirmation from the board members, my gaze swung to my mates. If anything happened to them, not even my newfound desire for peace could save the world from my wrath.

"Stay. Alive." I bit out, infusing as much grit into my tone as I could muster.

Yes, ma'am, Andrei whispered through our bond, a saucy look on his face. *Talk to me like that again in the bedroom later, baby girl.*

I had to hold back my eye roll, settling for a slight shake of my head as a smile touched my lips.

Tania drew my attention as she asked, "What if the slayers don't wish to broker a peace treaty? Not just the Devaroux House but the rest of the slayer population. What if they don't agree to meet?"

That was a possibility, and I don't have a Plan B.

Before I could admit to that, though, Drake cut in. He slid his elbows onto the table and propped his chin on top of his clasped hands as he considered Tania. "I've been thinking about that since you introduced your idea, Alina," he said as he turned his gaze to me. My brows rose, curiosity entirely piqued. "When Sanguis was established, one of the terms that was agreed upon was that we had to allow slayers to stay within our territory to build a civilization of their own."

I knew this, but I listened intently. It was crazy to me that I not only knew *the* Dracula who was there at the very beginning but that I was able to hear him recount it firsthand too.

"I'll have to double-check the records in my study, but I believe there was a stipulation in it that could help us. The stipulation stated that if laws and bylaws needed to be amended at any point, as long as the leader of one faction sent a handwritten letter expressing the need to do so to the other, the other was required to meet with them on neutral ground."

My eyes widened. "So they literally can't refuse to meet? That's great news."

"It's never been invoked by either side, and I will have to check the proper documents when this meeting has concluded to make sure. But yes, it's likely that they won't be able to refuse the meeting."

Lincoln tutted before asking, "But there's nothing that says a new agreement *must* be made, is there? We'd still need the leader of the slayers to agree to the new terms we bring them, correct?"

Drake let out a grunt, sitting back in his chair. "Correct."

The silence that followed was interrupted by a pinging sound. Drake fished his phone from his pocket, his brow furrowing as he read the message. His face turned gleeful as he flicked his eyes up to meet mine. "Priska is in. We just need to agree on a time and place, and Lo will convey it."

"Amazing," I breathed out, my shoulders sagged slightly. At least this part worked out. "Drake, can you look for those documents and bring back some parchment and ink from your office? Let's start the letter now, so we can send it quickly enough to reasonably establish that tomorrow is when we will have this meeting."

Drake nodded and slipped from the room, and I turned my attention back to planning with the others.

Half an hour later, after deciding on a small and trusted tactical team to accompany us to the meeting with the slayers, Heather, Tania, and Kiyomi were off.

Moments after the women left, all with a respectful dip of their chins in my direction, Drake returned with the parchment and ink and a pile of books. "It might take some time," he started as he dropped the books in the middle of the conference table, "I'd like to be able to reference the specific law in the letter."

It took hours and a lot of balled-up, failed drafts, but eventually, a piece of parchment covered in my sprawling black handwriting sat on the table staring back at me. We'd covered all our bases, and at this point, I felt like I was going cross-eyed at the number of books we'd sifted through to write dozens of letters until we got to this one. All that was left was for me to sign my name beside Drake's as the Queen of Sanguis.

My hand hovered over the parchment, the moment feeling so significant that the hair on my arms stood on end as I took a deep breath.

I didn't lift my eyes as I asked, my voice trembling slightly, "Can we really do this?"

There was no going back after this. We were opening doors that couldn't be closed, and the chance for bloodshed was high. Could I live with any more blood on my hands?

In a second, Drake was on his knee at my side, grabbing my chin and dragging my gaze to meet his eyes before releasing me. "The woman who just commanded this room believed in this plan. She believed in this vision for the future. She believed in all of us to help her achieve these unprecedented plans." His hand moved to lay over my heart. "Where did she go? Because the last time I checked, that woman was you."

Andrei moved to the chair Lo previously occupied on my right, grabbing my free hand and squeezing, pulling my gaze from Drake's intense stare. "We believe in you, Alina. We believe in these dreams for Sanguis."

"I knew the moment I saw you at DIA that my world was going to change," Lincoln said, grabbing my attention. I turned to look at him as he moved over one chair to sit in Drake's. The look he offered me, one filled with so much love and pride, left me feeling breathless. "What I didn't know was that you were not only going to change my life but the lives of everyone in Sanguis as well. I'm honored to have been chosen to be fated for a soul such as yours. To stand by your side as you strive to leave this land better than you found it is something I will never take for granted."

Each of their kind and supportive words lit my soul on fire until I felt like a blazing inferno of confidence, ready to take on the fucking world. My stomach fluttered at the future waiting for us. All I had to do was reach out and grab it.

My chest heaved with a deep breath as I nodded and blew it out. Tightening my grip on the quill in my hand, I dipped it in ink and found my designated spot. Drake had signed it simply as King Dracula, so perhaps I was only supposed to sign it as Queen Alina. I shook my head at the thought.

Dragging the tip along the paper, I didn't stop until the words Queen Alina Van Helsing were staring back at me in quickly drying ink.

Not long ago, all I had to cling to was my name. With no family, no friends, and no home, it was what got me through the really fucking hard times. I would never cower away from who I was.

Make them know your name, Soul Bond.

Each time Dev said that to me, it somehow felt different—bigger—than the last.

While you might have had the title since Drake appointed you and presented you to the board, you weren't truly ready for it. We both know that. But the woman who just signed that parchment? Queen Alina Van Helsing, indeed.

What would I do without you, Dev? I'm not sure what I did to deserve you, but I do know I couldn't have achieved everything I have without you.

It's not what you did to deserve me but what you're fated to do with me, Soul Bond. We were always fated to change the world.

Her words were powerful, hitting a deep chord inside of me that resonated outward until I was almost vibrating with the truth of them. I set the quill down and closed my eyes to soak in this moment, surrounded by those that loved me the most.

"We can fucking do this," I breathed.

As I opened my eyes, Drake pulled the parchment toward him and asked, "Are you ready for me to seal it with my crest and have it delivered?"

"Yes."

After alerting Tania that the letter was finally ready to be delivered, she came back to the castle. The letter was going to be delivered, and what was even better was the news that the tactical team had been briefed and was ready. As she turned to leave, I called out, "Tania, be safe. If they attempt anything while you're delivering it, get the hell out of there. I don't care if it doesn't make it to them, as long as you stay alive."

She glanced over her shoulder, smiling at me for the first time today. The gesture brought my own smile to my lips as she said, "I won't let you down, my queen."

With that, she was off, and there was nothing for us to do but wait for tomorrow to come. I glanced at the clock on the wall, finding that it was damn near six at night already. The meeting was set for noon the next day, so I had just enough time left to enjoy this evening with my mates before getting a good night of sleep.

"Take me back to our room. I want to soak in this night together before everything changes tomorrow."

They wasted no time doing as I asked, bringing me to the shower to pamper me before we fell into a pile on the bed. They ensured I knew just how loved I was by them, body and soul, before tucking me between their bodies to sleep. They murmured sweet nothings to me as my mind drifted off.

I feared my sleep would be filled with nightmares of all the awful outcomes that tomorrow could bring, but somehow it wasn't. Instead, I found myself lost in dreams of slayers and vampires living in a city together, one that boasted a bustling economy and ensured proper housing and education for all children, no matter their faction.

I dreamed of a society where no one had to live in fear.

CHAPTER TWENTY
ALINA

An hour before we were due to be at the designated spot, I found myself alone in the armory at the far end of the castle. My eyes took in each piece hungrily, my fingers running over the countless weapons and pieces of armor. Drake had an impressive collection, including shuriken, daggers, long swords, axes, spears, and guns.

Soon, the tactical team would come through here to gather what they needed. We had no idea what the response from House Devaroux or any of the slayers would be. Despite wanting this to be as peaceful as possible, I had to accept that I could be leading all these people into a battle where lives would be lost.

Everyone attending this meeting is a warrior, Alina. If someone falls today, on either side, they will have peace in knowing it wasn't worthless. It was for a cause they believed in until the end.

I drew to a halt at the table in the middle of the room, splaying my palms against the top and leaning my weight onto them. Forcing my eyes closed, I took a deep breath, filling my lungs until they hurt and holding it for a moment. After exhaling, when I didn't feel any of my nerves or uncertainty fading away, I repeated the process again. And then again and again until I felt steady enough.

You're right.

Of course I am.

A throat cleared behind me, causing me to whirl around. I prepared myself with the confident persona I needed to portray in front of the board members and tactical team, but when I saw who stood behind me, I deflated.

I closed the distance between us, throwing my arms around her neck as hers encircled my waist. My head fit atop hers from where she was tucked into my chest, and we just stood there, holding each other for a few moments.

"I fucking missed you," I said quietly, closing my eyes and soaking in this rare moment we had alone together. I had a feeling they would be fewer and farther between now. A dreamy sigh came from her, and I chuckled. "You didn't miss me at all, you bitch."

Truthfully, my words were filled with love for her and the situation she found herself in. She deserved to be spoiled in every damn way and feel like the most cherished treasure a partner had. From the glow radiating from her, Oleander had absolutely ensured that she felt like the center of his world.

There was still a little shock in my mind about the twist of fate we'd found ourselves in that brought the two of them together.

As she pulled back to look up at me, her eyes twinkled with mischief before she winked. "You know he's doing something right when I lose track of the days and can't even surface to send a text."

We dissolved into laughter and held each other once more before parting.

Her gaze lost its playful light as she turned serious, her eyebrows drawing together. "Drake told me there were a few rough days around here. Are you doing okay?"

A soft smile tilted the edges of my lips up as I nodded. "It was a breakdown that was a long time coming. For the first time since my life was turned upside down with the loss of my family, I feel like I'm learning how to live for myself. I'm no longer living the way I thought I had to, forcing myself to suffer to somehow justify that I got to live when none of them did. I wouldn't say my guilt for surviving is entirely gone, but I'm working on it."

"I'm so fucking proud of you, Al," she admitted, the conviction in her voice pouring out.

Before she could say anything further, Lincoln's head popped into the doorway. "Hey, do you have a quick second?"

My lips split into a full smile at the sight of him. "Of course. What's up?"

He sped over to me, pressing a wrinkled piece of paper into my hand. I shot him a questioning look after pulling it open to find a phone number on it and nothing else.

It's from Estrid. She said you could contact Alexandra this way.

My eyes widened as my lips parted. My gaze darted from him back to the paper over and over for a few seconds. Relief crashed into me as I closed the paper in my fist and held it to my chest.

This had to mean she was okay.

There haven't been any more deaths on campus

nor detection of threats around the land. According to Estrid, whatever Alexandra is doing is saving a hell of a lot of lives on campus and in Ordinarius.

While I was concerned about what she was facing, I knew that, like me, she had mates at her side who would fight tooth and nail for her safety. Pride blossomed within me with the knowledge that she was facing her demons head-on, just like I was today.

That's my fucking friend.

I'd like to meet her.

I mentally snorted. *Absolutely not. She's everything pure and light in this world. You'd corrupt her, you dirty, dirty little sword.*

She sassed me back instantly. **Oh, and you're saying you're oh-so innocent and pure now? Yeah fucking right.**

Grabbing Lincoln's hand and giving it a squeeze, I beamed up at him. *Thank you. I really needed this.*

After pressing a kiss to my forehead that made my toes curl, he turned to look between Lo and me. Holding out his elbows to us, he asked, "Tact team will be here in a moment. Shall we head to Drake, Andrei, and the other board members?"

As we both placed a hand in the crook of his elbows, I said, "We shall."

***

The dirt and rocks of the road crunched beneath my boots as we approached the southern border of our territory. It was the closest area we had to DIA, and while there was still quite some distance to the school, Lincoln assured us it was the most neutral area we had. It was also close enough that he could call Estrid for backup if shit hit the fan.

I had no intention of doing that, but knowing we had the option definitely put my nerves a bit more at ease.

Cresting the grassy hill, we drew to a halt as I caught sight of Jade's dark curls and bright blue eyes standing just behind her parents. The second our eyes met, she averted hers to the ground, and her father moved to block her from my view.

Confusion had my brows furrowing, but I shook it off, forcing myself to focus on the important details. Their group stood off to the side of the tent we had arranged to put up overnight. A table with room for five people from each side sat in the middle. Glancing toward the slayers, I realized I had no idea who would sit on their side besides Jade and her parents.

I quickly counted nearly forty slayers backing the three of them, which meant there was a mixture of several Houses present. To my knowledge, the House of Devaroux only had around twenty members.

We had twenty skilled tactical team members who stood behind our group. With my mates, the board, and Priska at my back, I had faith that if the meeting led to a fight, we would be able to take them. Even with the numbers skewed in their favor.

Damn straight, we can.

Narrowing my eyes on the slayers behind Jade and her parents, I scanned them for faces I would recognize, instantly regretting that decision when my eyes landed on a pair of cold grey ones that were framed by blonde hair and attached to a small frame.

Skye had always been the spitting image of her mother, and the sight of Bethany had my knees trembling. No part of me planned on having to face Skye's parents during this. Undoubtedly, I knew one day I would have to, but right now... My gut churned, bile threatening to come up my throat.

Would they be sitting at the table with House Devaroux?

Drake slipped his hand into mine, squeezing lightly and centering my spiraling thoughts with the small gesture.

Ready for this, Comoroă?

With a deep breath and the knowledge that what I was trying to accomplish here would hopefully prevent senseless deaths like Skye's, I lifted my chin high and walked forward with all my mates at my side.

Yes.

I couldn't erase the past or bring Skye back, but I could look her parents in the eye as I exposed the truth of that dreadful night and proved to them that I wasn't the same slayer who ran away. I was a woman who'd grown from her sorrow and traumas and was resolved to never run away again. I would stand before them, proud of the person I'd fought to become despite the odds being stacked against me.

Not bothering to speak with the slayers until they decided to also be civil, we headed directly for the table, taking the seats we arranged last night. I sat in the center, with Drake on my right and Priska on my left. Lincoln sat to the left of Priska as her guard, and Andrei to the right of Drake.

As we waited for the slayers to approach and take their seats, Priska's hand found my left knee, giving me a few gentle taps of support as she leaned into my side. Her sweet lemongrass scent wrapped around me. "Remember, one squeeze for truth, two for a lie."

For someone who stated they wanted nothing to do with political affairs, when I met her this morning, she exuded excitement over our need for her at this meeting. It turned out that all she needed was the right cause to support. Her excitement for this turn in our society gave me hope that perhaps I wasn't going to be met with as much resistance by the vampires as I initially thought.

Glancing into her shimmering, almost opalescent eyes, I gave her a smile and nod in confirmation. Her gaze flew toward the slayers as the sound of their approach carried on the wind, her black hair whipping around her at the sudden movement.

I took a deep, steadying breath before slowly moving my attention toward them as well, mentally preparing myself for my nightmares to come true.

And they absolutely did.

Jade's father, Alix, took a seat in front of me, with her mom, Laura, in front of Drake. Jade sat in front of Andrei. Skye's mother, Bethany, sat to the left of Alix, with her father, Richard, on the far side across from Lincoln.

I refused to cower before them, meeting each of

their eyes as I welcomed them. "Thank you for meeting us on short notice. We appreciate your willingness to discuss new terms for the laws existing in Sanguis."

Alix's dark eyes narrowed as he snapped, "We are only here because that is the law we must follow as slayers. Unlike you, we hold to our laws and rules."

I felt the vibrations of feral anger pouring through my bonds, and I sent soothing waves of calmness back to them, assuring them that his words didn't bother me.

"Do not take our presence here as a willingness to make changes to our laws. They work as is, and we have no desire to see them changed in favor of the vampires," he spat out, venom dripping from his words.

He didn't have an inkling of an idea of what I wanted to change, and if he did, he'd jump at the chance for slayers to have more power than they do now. As it was, this was the vampire's territory, and the slayers were only allowed within it as a policing group. He was such an ignorant fool.

I held his gaze, keeping my face devoid of emotion, as I thought back to the respectful and kind man I'd seen him as growing up. He doted on

Jade endlessly and never made me feel like he wasn't supportive of our friendship.

Was he always this monster deep down? If so, he was as excellent an actor as Jeoffrey was on the board. Funny how it was becoming more apparent to me every day how fucking corrupt the world around us was, no matter what side someone claimed to support.

When he settled back into his chair, having leaned over the table as he shoved his finger at me during his little tirade, I waited a second before raising a single eyebrow at him. My tone was cool and collected as I asked, "Did you get that all out of your system, or did you need to waste a few more minutes of our time by acting like you have any idea of what we are here to propose?"

Shock and pride flitted through my bonds, and I kept my chin raised when Alix's gaze turned to one of pure fury as he stared back at me. I refused to look away or cower from him. I'd stared into the eyes of many monsters and won, and that wasn't about to change now.

"You dare speak to the ruling House representative like that?" he hissed. His dig at taking the title from my family was not subtle at all.

I couldn't help but let out a little chuckle,

smirking before I rebutted, "You dare speak to the Queen of the lands you occupy like that?"

Bethany shoved to her feet, her blonde hair dancing around her in the wind blowing over us. Tears streamed down her cheeks as she hissed, "You dare call yourself a queen after the atrocities you've committed? Do you have no remorse for your sins?"

I felt the anguish in her voice, and unlike with Alix, there wasn't an underlying superiority complex attached to it. This was solely about her child's life being ripped away from her, and for that, I would offer her a true response.

"I spent weeks after leaving my home and everyone I knew hating the monster I thought I'd become. All I did was try to find a path that would lead me to the completion of my blood oath to get vengeance on the people behind the attack on my family and, in turn, the loss of Skye through my transition."

Alix grinned out of the corner of my eye, and I ached to call forth Devorare and point the tip of my blade at his throat.

Richard cut in, his grey eyes cold as he shook his head at me. "And how exactly have you accomplished that? All I see is a child given a crown that she has no right to bear."

I took their biting words gracefully, knowing they only had a narrow perspective of the situation. That was about to change.

Before I could answer, Drake cut in with a voice like ice, and chills coated my body as he warned, "Do not mistake our silence as acceptance for the way you are speaking to our mate right now. I strongly suggest you monitor your words moving forward before our decorum and politeness fly out of the window right behind your own."

The reminder of who was at my side forced Bethany back into her seat, her mouth snapping closed. Brushing my hand over Drake's knee in thanks, I shifted my gaze to Alix and his suspiciously quiet wife. Under the weight of my focus, she shifted in her chair, refusing to meet my eyes.

I shifted my gaze to Jade and found her looking down at the table. She had never been a subdued or quiet woman, always quick to defend Skye and me if anyone dared fuck with us. I didn't recognize this version of her, and it made my heart squeeze with confusion.

Perhaps my questions about their situation would be answered at the same time I asked my questions to her parents.

Fixing my stare back on Alix, I announced,

"Before we begin discussing the new changes we'd like to implement, we want to ensure we are speaking with the correct representative of the slayers. I, for one, know that the ruling House must be backed by all within our territory to hold that title."

Laura spoke up then, snapping at me, "You need not throw our own rules in our face. We know them, and we do have the backing of everyone."

I let my eyes narrow, and my fangs lengthen as I smiled. "But do they know who they're backing and what you've done to gain power? It's time we lay out all the facts to ensure that is the case."

Jade's head snapped up to me, eyes wide and lips parted as her gaze bounced back and forth between me and her parents. "What does she mean by that?" Her voice was the fine edge of a sharp sword as she demanded information from her parents.

There was some of that fire I knew was within her.

"I have a list of specific questions for you both," I continued, tilting my head to the side as I enjoyed watching their skin pale. "And you will be answering *to me.*"

CHAPTER TWENTY-ONE
ALINA

Alix bristled, top lip pulling up in a snarl as he pushed to his feet. "We do not have to subject ourselves to an interrogation led by *you*. Laura, Jade, we're leaving now."

My response was clipped as I also stood in a rush, placing my hands flat on the table and leaning over it. "If you have nothing to hide, why are you running like you're guilty before even hearing my questions?"

Laura jumped to her feet, slipping her hand into her husband's elbow. She tugged on it as he stood there, holding my gaze with hatred dripping from every pore on his body. "Honey, let's go. Now," she ground out through gritted teeth, and I noticed that she was desperately trying to avoid my eyes.

Alix refused to budge from or surrender in this battle of wills clashing between us, leaving us in a limbo of crackling energy.

"Sit down."

The quiet command came from the end of the table, but there was enough bite to the words to grind everyone to a halt as our eyes were pulled in that direction.

Jade's eyes met mine before roaming over my face like she was searching for something. If I knew what she wanted to know, I'd give it to her in a heartbeat. There was something vulnerable about the way her eyes widened and the way she took in a deep breath. With my enhanced hearing, I picked up on the shakiness of her breath, which only hit me in the gut that much harder.

Deep in the depths of those bright blue eyes was my best friend—the one I'd considered my sister. The one my soul still yearned for. With the loss of my family and Skye, I'd somehow been blessed with a path that led me to my mates, Lo, Alexandra, and now Serena. They were my found family, and yet my heart still claimed Jade as a part of that group.

Her lip quivered as I tried to convey all of those big, conflicting feelings through my eyes, willing her to feel my love for her still. It was at this moment that my heart decided once and for all that Jade wasn't a part of what happened between our families. She couldn't be. The love we held for each other was pure and real. It couldn't have been a facade, and if it wasn't, she would never hurt me like that.

It was a fact I'd tried so vehemently to deny and why I had clung so fucking hard to my fury for her and her family that the thought of coming after them consumed me for too long. Nothing in me was capable of lifting a finger against her—not when all I wanted to do was drag her into my arms and figure out how to mend the rift between us.

I wanted my sister back.

"Jade, get up," Alix seethed, breaking the trance between us in favor of staring daggers at his daughter.

All at once, the vulnerability in her eyes vanished as her attention slid from me to her father, instead turning into a blazing fire of determination.

Hope sparked within my chest when I saw that look on her face. She was the most stubborn person I knew, which was saying a lot. The scathing look she was giving her father meant she was actually going to hear me out and no one would convince her otherwise.

"Sit. Down. Now." She rebutted in a clipped

tone, lifting her chin and putting her gorgeous, sharp features on display as the wind blew her hair away from her face. "I'm not leaving this meeting until I hear these questions and answers. You have evaded me at home for far too long now."

I swear my heart came to a screeching halt in my chest with her admission. Why were her parents evading her at home?

Suddenly, her quiet presence and the way Alix and Laura seemed to try to keep her from speaking up made sense. She was already asking questions about that night. Part of her was unsettled about it and fighting to find the truth.

My throat squeezed as I fought back the hopeful tears that threatened to spring up in my burning eyes.

She hadn't given up on me.

I felt a gentle squeeze on my left knee, Priska silently letting me know that Jade was telling the truth. All at once, the possibilities of the implications of her words poured through my mind.

Skye's parents stood to their feet ever so slowly, shoulders pulled back and displaying spines of steel as they faced Alix and Laura.

It was a clear display of support for Jade, with them still hating my guts, but I would take them transitioning to a somewhat neutral party over just having their wrath.

"I suggest you sit down and answer the questions, Alix," Bethany said as her husband's hand came to rest on her shoulder in support. "Unless you'd like us to assume your guilt in whatever Alina wants to ask you about. We would have no choice but to withdraw our support of your House."

Even them saying my name without scalding animosity felt like a major victory.

I could have bulldozed my way into the conversation and prattled off what I knew at that point, but *this* was exactly why I'd chosen to take a diplomatic approach. If I'd let out the headstrong, take no prisoners version of myself I operated as before my breakdown, I would have looked like an accusatory and aggressive lunatic.

In being able to control my emotions and keep a cool head, I was allowing everyone here the opportunity to draw their own conclusions.

Alix's chest puffed out, cheeks reddening with anger as he waved a hand in the air. "This is ridiculous! I am not guilty of anything other than not wanting to be interrogated by someone who betrayed our kind. I owe her nothing."

My chest heaved as I forced myself to take in the

most steadying and calming breath I'd ever drawn in my life. He owed me *everything*.

My back straightened, and I squared my shoulders as I cut him off before he could continue his indignant tirade. "You do actually owe me this. You owe me a hell of a lot more than this, and what I want more than anything, you can't possibly give me. I want my family, Alix."

My heart hammered in my chest, my anger rising to levels that I was struggling to suppress at the absolute disregard in his words. Blood whooshed in my ears as I felt a bloodhaze threatening the edge of my consciousness.

"Shall we get started?" Priska asked from my side, gesturing to their chairs with her hand. "I'm sure we all have a lot to do with our days. Let's get this over with, so we can return to our lives."

Her tone was placating enough that Alix and Laura managed to put a damper on their rampaging emotions, shooting me scathing looks before pulling their masks back on and dropping back into their seats. Skye's parents quickly followed suit.

I felt fingers tapping on my leg, and a wave of soothing emotions flowed through me. The sensation was like a river of water running slowly through a forest fire, sizzling with steam as the two opposing forces met but eventually gave way.

The red that tinged the edge of my vision faded, and I was able to take my seat.

I owed Priska my profuse gratitude for offering me her calming energy. While I was actively trying to turn over a new leaf and not let my emotions control my actions, I wasn't perfect.

All at once my mate's voices flew into my mind alongside their warmth and support.

Keep pushing, baby girl.

I'm so proud of you, Spitfire.

Comoroă, I wish you could see the exquisite and regal queen that you are from our perspective . Do not falter. Get your answers.

I tried to fight the smile that threatened but gave up quickly, knowing it would downright piss Alix and Laura off. The edges of my lips turned up in glee, and right on cue, red splotches began to creep up Alix's cheeks all the way to the tips of his ears.

Fuck. That felt so good.

"Now then," I huffed, feeling renewed in my determination after the reassurances of my mates. "Before I start my line of questions, I'd like to inform everyone present that if anyone is found guilty of crimes, we intend to process those persons through a trial as part of our new government. The jury and judges will be an equal mix of vampires and slayers."

I wasn't sure why my eyes fell on Jade as I made my announcement. Her reaction shouldn't have mattered to me so fucking much, but I thought her opinion would probably always matter to me this much. Jade didn't leave me waiting long, her mouth popping open in shock alongside a gasp from the other side of the table from Bethany.

I couldn't dwell on her reaction, though. Instead, I pushed forward with my first question, not willing to allow the conversation to be derailed again. "Alix and Laura, did you have prior knowledge of the plan to attack the Van Helsing House on the night of their deaths?"

Alix's answer was quick and cold, smothering the sharp inhales of breath from Skye's parents, who seemed to finally see where I was going with this. "No."

Two squeezes to my knee. *Lie.*

I had to swallow down the bubble of fury when Priska confirmed the Devarouxs' knowledge of the attack. It was what I expected, but it didn't take away the sting of pain that accompanied the answer.

It was only going to get worse from here, and I

didn't want to give away Priska's power until I had all of my answers, so I forged on.

"Did you have contact with the previous Knight on Dracula's Board named Jeoffrey? Specifically, did you make a deal with him to attack the Van Helsing house in an effort to wipe us out to give you a chance at becoming the ruling House?"

Laura answered this time, holding her head high as she did. "Of course not. First, we would never stoop so low as to—"

I held up a hand, cutting off her rambling as I let condescension drip from my tone now that I had my truth. "It is a simple yes or no question, Laura. I don't need your life story."

Her nostrils flared as she spat, "No."

I wasn't at all surprised to feel another two squeezes to my knee.

I didn't let off the pressure, rapidly firing my next question.

"Did you hire a witch to deconstruct a specified section of the magical barrier around the slayer's home in order to allow the vampires under Jeoffrey's control to carry out the attack *and* have an escape route?"

At this point, Alix's face was the color of a ripe tomato. As our eyes clashed once more, I thought he was going to crack a tooth with how tightly he clenched his jaw.

"As stated before," he ground out, unclenching his jaw just enough to speak, "we did not know of the attack on your family before it happened, so how—".

I relished in this moment as I held my hand up again, keeping my tone even as I sighed. "And as I told your wife, it's a simple yes or no question. I don't need your endless drivel."

He shot to his feet, looking ready to spill my blood and bathe in it. Before he could make a move, Drake was at his back after a blur of speed, shoving him back down into the chair. The force of the movement was so harsh I heard a crack of wood and half expected the chair to crumble beneath Alix's weight.

My eyes narrowed, my heart in my chest at the contact. Their reinforcements were in clear view of the tent, and despite not having enhanced hearing, they would have no issue seeing Drake's move.

It felt like we collectively held our breath as Drake patted him on the back and slowly began the walk back to our side of the table with a sigh. "If everyone could just remain in their chairs for the duration of the meeting, we won't have further problems. I know baby vampires that can sit still longer than this bunch."

"Touch me again, and we *will* have further problems," Alix warned, gaze narrowed on Drake's back.

Jade tensed as Drake passed her, but she kept her eyes on me, seemingly waiting for my next question. Sorrow hit me, because the remainder of my questions for her parents really weren't for me anymore...They were for her.

Realizing that I needed to let Jade in on how we would know if their answers were the truth or not, I bit my lip before sighing and addressing her parents again.

"Alix, Laura," I said in a no-nonsense tone, pulling the focus back to me. "Priska here is from a rare bloodline of vampires that can sense people's emotions without touching them. She is the strongest one in existence, and she has the ability to sense whether someone is lying or not, hence the questions we've been asking you."

Richard stuttered, "H-How did we not know of that? It's not in any of our history books."

Priska answered for herself, quickly explaining, "My family doesn't like to make ourselves known. We prefer to silently help people in need over doing anything to deserve fame. This meeting is worth losing our anonymity. Would you like a display of my powers?"

He quickly nodded, not missing a beat as he gestured to me, "Ask me anything."

My brain sputtered momentarily at being put on the spot. All the questions that came to mind were about Skye, the one person that Bethany, Richard, Jade and I would all know like the back of our hand. It needed to be something to prove Priska's power to us all.

My voice softened as I asked, "What was Skye's favorite color?"

His throat bobbed as he swallowed before glancing to the table and whispered, "Teal."

We all knew that was wrong. It was pink. The girl had been obsessed with all shades of pink and didn't hide it. She was the real princess in my life, the total opposite to my strictly black wardrobe back then.

"Lie," Priska quickly said before asking, "anything further?"

No one answered, and a melancholy silence descended over the group, save for my two targets. I saw the anger Laura and Alix had exhibited beginning to morph into unfiltered fear. Their throats bobbed as their eyes shifted around, likely scoping out the best chance for escape.

Knowing we had only a limited amount of time remaining, I quickly asked, "Did you use your daughter as a pawn to get me exactly where you needed me in order to fulfill your goal that night?"

CHAPTER TWENTY-TWO
ALINA

They froze, fidgeting hands falling to rest on the table as their faces went slack.

Truthfully, I wasn't sure how they felt about Jade. Did they care about her? Were they trying to protect her by not telling her to keep her hands clean? Or were they just using her? Did they think she wasn't capable enough to assist them without their deception?

Did they even care what Jade thought of them? I had to think so if they went to such lengths to keep her in the dark.

Silence stretched as their eyes darted around the tent, looking anywhere but at me now. As their shock about Priska wore off and they realized the position I had put them in, I could, without a doubt, say I'd never had anyone look at me with such fiery hatred as they were when their eyes landed on me.

"Answer the question," I demanded softly.

I wanted them to look me in the eye and tell me what pieces of shit they were now that they knew I would know if they lied.

"No," Laura breathed out in response, her answer barely even audible to my enhanced hearing.

I shook my head at their inability to speak the truth. They'd be liars until they died, incapable of facing their own truths, it seemed.

Tears lined Laura's eyes as Priska loudly announced, "You said no, and that is a *lie.*"

A scream of agony ripped from Jade's throat, and I could see the second the shrill scream alerted their reinforcements that something had gone wrong, though they misunderstood the situation. When their forces deployed, ours did as well, putting us directly in the middle of a battle that did not need to happen.

Shit was about to hit the fucking fan, and instead of letting my fear overwhelm me, I remained calm and made quick commands to my mates.

Andrei and you need to grab Laura and Alix. They will use the confusion to try to escape, I sent to Drake. *I'm grabbing Jade.*

Lincoln already knew his job was to protect Priska and needed no direction from me.

We had approximately thirty seconds before this was unsalvageable.

"Stop your forces," I demanded, but Alix simply smiled back at me.

My eyes flickered to Jade, who pushed up from her chair, seemingly in a daze. My heart leapt to my throat as she walked directly toward our tactical team.

They were faster than the slayers, and I had a quick decision to make. Did I call them off and risk taking on the slayers without them?

She took a few more stumbling steps, and I hissed, "Damn it," as I flashed over to block her body with my own. I whirled to face our team, which was led by the board members.

It wasn't even a question. I'd fight an entire army alone if it meant keeping Jade out of harm's way. I wouldn't let anyone take a single member of my remaining family from me.

Holding up a hand, I sought out Lo at the front and yelled, "Stop!"

The group halted immediately at my command, but I saw shuffling feet and indecision in the eyes of a few of the vampires as they lowered their weapons to the ground. The rest of the team kept their eyes locked on the slayers approaching behind me. I felt the ground shaking beneath my feet as they approached. My vampires had to trust me.

Lo gave me a nod as I felt Jade sag against my back, her hands wrapping around my waist as her sobs rang loudly in my ears.

"Alina, I'm so sorry," she sobbed. I had to force myself to not look at her because I knew if I did, I'd be a fucking wreck right alongside her. The tearful reunion had to wait. I needed to make sure we were all safe right now.

I quickly spun and grabbed Jade, moving her from my back to my side. Keeping my arm wrapped firmly around her, I held her to me as she put more and more of her weight on me.

What I found behind me shocked me.

Drake and Andrei had Jade's parents pinned against the table with handcuffs on their wrists. But that wasn't what had my eyes widening and tears blurring my vision.

Richard and Bethany had pulled their soul weapons out, showcasing a beautiful scythe and a bow. Both weapons were trained on the approaching slayers, who slowed to a halt as Bethany called out, "If anyone tries to help Laura or

Alix, I won't hesitate in taking your head. Please, show me who dared support them in their heinous crimes. I'd love to rid this world of a few more monsters today."

Holy shit. She was defending us. A lone tear tracked down my cheek at the sight of her standing there in the face of slayers to defend vampires, the very creatures she'd come to this meeting with nothing but hatred in her heart for.

I heard footsteps approaching behind me, and I glanced over my shoulder to see Lincoln and Priska at the front of the tactical team alongside Lo and the board. They all slowly inched closer. Now that the lines in the sand were drawn, I knew Lincoln and Lo would ensure they didn't harm the slayers who were on our side.

"Unhand me!" Alix yelled, trying to buck Drake off. Meanwhile, his wife was slumped like a dejected husk of herself, completely limp and folded over the table as her gaze was locked on Jade.

For a tense moment, both sides just stood there, staring. As Jade found her strength to stand up next to me, the eyes of the slayers brought from House Devaroux turned toward her.

She wiped the tears from her blotchy face, sniffling, before putting her hand into mine and squeezing. Instinctively, I gripped her hand back, part of me afraid that this was just a dream and I wouldn't be able to hold on to her for very long at all.

Her chin raised as she looked at her family and decreed in a wobbly voice, "My parents are traitors to House Devaroux. They have been found guilty of orchestrating the murders of House Van Helsing, working in conjunction with vampires and witches to ensure their downfall."

She gained confidence as she went on, her voice leveling out as she took a deep breath and continued, "They will be put to trial for their crimes, and a jury of slayers and vampires will decide their fate."

Gasps and murmured whispers came from the group, but still, they stood down, lowering their weapons. As soon as they did, my shoulders sagged in relief.

As Drake and Andrei hauled her parents toward our tactical team, passing them off with strict instructions on where to put them upon our return, Jade turned to me and threw her arms around my neck. This time, I was able to properly return the embrace without fear for our lives.

She held onto me tightly as she said, "I was so blinded by my own fear and feelings of betrayal when I found you and Skye. As soon as you left, all I did was replay the evening over and over again in my head, Alina. I should have never treated you the way I did that night." Her voice cracked as she continued, "At the time, I thought I had lost you both. I thought you were lost in the shell of a monster that was staring back at me."

It hurt to hear Jade's admissions, but holding her in my arms and being able to have this talk soothed the pain.

I squeezed her a little tighter as I whispered back, "I don't blame you, Jade. I could sit here and say that I wouldn't have reacted the same way. But the truth is that we were raised to see things as black and white. In that moment, I was the monster we were raised to kill."

It hit me then how astounding it was that, despite the vile things she said to me that night, she still let me go. She'd refused to kill me, despite my begging her for it. I'd always seen it as a selfish decision on her part, but as we stood here together now, I realized it was the most selfless decision she could have made. Jade went against our laws as slayers and let me live.

It was almost like she could read my mind as she admitted, "I couldn't do it. I couldn't give you what you begged of me that night. A part of me always hoped we'd somehow find our way back to one another, despite being pitted against each other after that night."

As I pulled back to stare into her eyes, I reached up to brush away her tears before cupping her face. "I love you, Jade. You're still my family despite everything that has happened in between then and now."

A hesitant smile pulled at her lips. "I know we have *a lot* to discuss, but do you think that I could maybe stay with you tonight?"

Her question shocked me, and I couldn't help but lower my voice and ask, "You do realize that means you would be surrounded by a bunch of vampires with no other slayers in sight, right?"

A tinkling laugh fell from her lips as she nodded, squeezing my arms. "Yes, Alina. You are the queen of the vampires, after all."

My heart melted as I realized that she really wanted that.

With an enthusiastic nod, I moved to guide her toward my mates and Lo.

My old life and my new life were finally about to meet. For once, the thought brought me nothing but joy. An all-encompassing euphoria soared within my soul.

A faint flutter in my heart brought me to a stop, and Jade faltered at my side. Our heads whipped around, our gazes clashing.

"Did you feel that?" she questioned, brows drawn together.

Just then, the scent of cherry blossoms flowed through the air despite no trees being present here, and my eyes watered. Jade sniffled, her own eyes watery with emotion.

"Skye," I whispered, glancing around for her despite knowing it wasn't possible.

I can sense other souls, and hers is here with you now, just as your parents were briefly the other night.

My hand found Jade's, threading our fingers together as my lip wobbled with sorrow. I had one of my sisters back, but I'd never have Skye again. I'd never be able to take back that night, no matter if I was manipulated into the situation.

Warmth surrounded me, as if the air was hugging me, and a sob ripped out of my throat as my tears fell. Glancing at Jade, I whispered, "It's her."

Jade's eyes closed as she nodded, her own tears falling down her cheeks. Her voice cracked, "I feel her too."

Guilt gnawed at my heart, but Dev's words were firm and full of love, as I felt Skye's energy surround me.

She wants you to live a life full of love and laughter and to honor her memory with smiles, not tears.

"Shit," I hissed, furiously wiping away my tears with my free hand. "I'm doing a really fucking bad job of that, aren't I, Skye?"

I closed my eyes and soaked in her warmth, recalling our incredible memories together until my tears finally stopped, and a smile pulled at my lips.

The only person you still need forgiveness from is yourself, Alina. Are you ready to do that once and for all?

With a deep inhale and exhale, I opened my eyes and looked around at the beautiful souls I was lucky enough to be surrounded by before gazing into the sky.

"I am."

EPILOGUE I
ALINA

Seven months later

A laugh burst out of me as I waited to walk across the stage to get my diploma.

"De Luca, give me the microphone back," Lincoln hissed, wrestling Andrei on the stage in front of not only our entire graduating class but graduates from every sector and all of our loved ones as well.

I exchanged a smirk with Drake, who had, of course, used his position as king to ensure he was front and center at the ceremony, sitting with all the other professors of DIA.

They're a mess.

But they're our mess.

Andrei doubled over with Lincoln on his back, finally getting the microphone close enough to his lips to yell, "I just want everyone to know that Professor Lincoln is my very best friend and wears my friendship bracelet every day!"

I had to lift my hands to smother the absolute monstrosity of a laugh that threatened to spill out of me. If I let it out, I just knew it was going to be a mix of a snort, a cackle, and a howl. No one needed to hear that.

With a growl, Lincoln finally ripped the microphone back into his hand and stood up. He straightened his clothes and heaved a deep sigh as Andrei walked off the stage, waiting on the other side for me with a beaming grin on his handsome face.

Running a hand down his disheveled suit once more, Lincoln cleared his throat and picked up the next diploma before turning his gaze to me, his hazel eyes smoldering pits of gold and green. And he stood there, licking his lips like he hadn't had his *breakfast* just a few hours ago.

You look stunning, Princess, but I want to rip the eyes out of every person who is about to see you in that dress.

I'd gone back and forth over what to wear about

a hundred times before finally settling on Lo and Jade's mutual choice. I wore a simple black satin midi dress that hugged all my curves nicely without being obscene like some of the other overly tight options I'd had. Pairing it with strappy heels that tied up around my ankle and red lipstick, and opting to only wear my engagement ring as jewelry, I called it a day.

Heat crept up my chest and my cheeks as he pulled the microphone to his mouth and announced, "The last graduate from the vampire sector of Dark Imaginarium Academy is someone incredibly special. My mate, my future wife, and the Queen of Sanguis—Alina Van Helsing."

Cheers erupted, startling me. Lincoln had warned me that news of our accomplishments and the massive change in Sanguis had trickled back to the school. Honestly, it felt like overnight I went from being the reject of our sector to suddenly having everyone wanting to talk to me.

It took some time to find a happy medium between being polite and interacting with people while still protecting my peace. I loved my core group of people and simply didn't have the mental spoons to let anyone else in right now. With my little family alone, we already had so much on our plates with our new jobs that I barely felt like I had time to see them as it was.

As I forced myself to begin the walk across the stage, I kept my eyes on Lincoln, hating to be the center of attention like this. My dreams last night were plagued with an endless loop of me tripping in my heels and becoming known as the woman who couldn't even cross a stage without falling on her face.

The anxiety began to creep up, and my eyes began to stray toward the audience, but Lincoln was quick to pull my focus back to him.

Come to me, Princess.

I nibbled on my lip as he reached out his hand, and relief crashed through me as our skin touched, slipping my hand into his. *This* was the magic that each of my bonds gave me. I'd yet to face anything that I couldn't accomplish as long as I had their love and support behind me.

He leaned in to press a kiss on my cheek before passing me my diploma. We turned and posed for the standard picture together by the photographer off to the side, near Andrei. He gave me two thumbs up, making me smile way too hard for the photo, but I didn't care. I wasn't ever going to let my emotions be squashed again.

I wanted to feel everything—hard. I'd wasted too much time trying to fit into the mold of the perfect slayer, and all I wanted to be now was *me*.

I glanced at Estrid in her spot behind the diploma table, looking as stunning and put together as ever with her white pencil skirt and red satin blouse, and gave her a small wave. I grabbed Lincoln's hand to head over to say goodbye to her, but he refused to budge, staying in his spot.

I gave him a questioning look, my brows drawing together, before glancing at Andrei and then Drake, but they shrugged their shoulders.

Estrid's heels clicked over the stage as she moved to stand on Lincoln's other side, clearly in on whatever was happening here. As she stared at him with adoration and tears forming in her eyes, my anxiety doubled.

As he raised the microphone to his mouth once more, he inhaled deeply and glanced around the pavilion in the center of DIA. When his eyes landed on Estrid again, he blew the breath out before speaking. "I wanted to take a moment to acknowledge how special Dark Imaginarium Academy has been for me. I came here as a jaded young adult, unsure of what the future held for me, but for some reason, our headmistress saw something within me and decided to take a chance on me."

Estrid quickly wiped a few tears away before she smiled widely.

Lincoln's gaze swung back to the gate to our sector, and he squeezed my hand tightly before continuing, "While I was brought here to teach future generations of vampires, this academy taught me a lot of my own hard lessons and shaped me into the man that I am today. I'll always remember where I came from, and DIA will always be the first home I found, but I must say goodbye to it now as I take on my new role as co-head-master of the new academy in Sanguis. Thank you all."

My jaw dropped as cheers and rounds of applause filled the air.

Jade had been begging Lincoln to take on that position with her for months, overwhelmed with handling administration, vetting instructors, and everything else as the construction of the academy drew to a close. There wasn't a better person for the job, and I knew the decision had been plaguing him for months now.

He passed the microphone to Estrid, who had to clear her throat a few times before she said, "Just like we say to all our graduates: You will always have a home here at DIA. Go make us proud."

Lincoln let go of my hand briefly to wrap Estrid in a tight hug. The moment felt like watching the student become equal to the master, with him now taking on the title of headmaster himself.

Next school year, we would be welcoming our first class of recruits, open to both slayers and vampires. The only applicants we would allow would be those who had aspirations of joining the new task force Andrei and I were heading for Sanguis. We'd dissolved the current tactical teams after growing pains became apparent in our desire to mesh the two communities.

The academy was intended to be the starting place to overcome prejudices between vampires and slayers. The goal was to learn how to work as a cohesive unit when there were differences in strength and previous training and prejudices obscuring their minds, but once they graduated, they would be given a placement on one of the teams protecting our new integrated society.

As the crowd began to disperse with the ceremony over, Andrei and Drake came to stand beside me as Estrid and Lincoln shared a private conversation.

I gave them each a peck before looking at Drake's new beard, remembering just how much I loved it when it was buried between my legs and scratching deliciously against my thighs. It had grown past the usual stubble he wore due to the stress forming the new council, and I'd *begged* for it to become a permanent thing.

The Sanguis Council came into being after dissolving what was left of the board. It was a fresh start, consisting of the four trusted ex-board members who remained and a representative from each slayer House. Their first task was to field hire requests from the other territories in Praeditus for our upcoming enforcement teams, and we already had a substantial waitlist, to my utter shock.

"Don't you dare look at me like that right now, *Comoroă*," Drake warned, his tone husky despite his words of warning. "That sinful dress of yours has your little friend wanting to make good on our promise to take you wherever we want, whenever we want."

A smirk tugged at my lips at the way he referred to his monster as my little friend now. We'd become very well acquainted.

Andrei cleared his throat, subtly adjusting his cock and making me laugh before he groaned and said, "I have to go check on the house after this. The contractor said that we're looking at at least another month before we can officially move in."

Lincoln joined us then, tossing his arm around my shoulder as he sighed. "That house is going to give me grey hairs."

Drake rolled his eyes. "Don't even. I will pull the old age card all day."

A rumble of laughter spread through my chest as I shook my head at them. "The wait for the house will be worth it," I cooed in a placating tone. "You can't rush perfection. This is our forever home, after all."

"I can absolutely rush it when you won't even discuss our wedding plans until it's done," Drake growled, earning nods of agreement from Lincoln and Andrei.

My mouth dropped open, and I held my hand to my chest as I vehemently defended my choice. "It's the perfect space for our wedding! I want the first day of our new lives together to be the very best day of our lives. Is that too much to ask for?"

They acted like I was planning to make them wait ten years to marry me, but their complaints about the wait warmed my heart every time. Their excitement to officially claim me as their wife was something I'd never get tired of.

Lincoln's lips fell to my ear as he whispered, "Nothing is too much to ask for, Princess. You know we'd give you the world and more if you only asked."

And they really would.

How did I get so damn lucky?

EPILOGUE 2
ALINA

Two years later

My shot glass cracked as I slammed it down, maybe with a bit too much force, onto the vanity in our bedroom. The room had been transformed into the bridal suite for today, and somehow I felt both at ease and nervous in the familiar space. "Another," I demanded, cursing that my tolerance was ridiculously high as a vampire.

Lo poured both herself and me another shot of tequila after replacing my glass with a fresh, non-cracked one. She chuckled as she did so.

Jade groaned as she flopped back onto the bed behind me. "Fuck, there's no way I can keep up with you both if I want there to be any hope of me remembering the day."

I shared a mischievous look with Lo as she poured a third shot.

It had become clear as we developed our friendship that Lo and I were absolutely not to be trusted. Thankfully, Jade and Alexandra still loved us anyway.

Lo danced over to Jade before crawling onto the bed and holding the shot over her mouth, pleading with her in a whiny baby voice to try to get Jade to take another. My eyes pricked with tears at the sight, though laughter bubbled from my lips.

I felt beyond blessed that the two of them quickly welcomed each other into their lives and began building their own friendship without me having to be the anchor for it. Even when everything felt too fucking hard while merging our two communities, these two brought my hope rushing back to the forefront of my mind.

It hadn't been as easy to see Alexandra with her new position, but every time she'd been able to stop by, it was like a missing piece of the puzzle fit right into place every time. I loved that about our friendship. It didn't matter the amount of time that went between seeing or talking to each other, we always picked up right where it left off.

The horrendous trial of Jade's parents, as well as a few more of her family members who had been outed for having a hand in the attack on my family, had dragged on for six months. But in the end, they were found guilty and sentenced. Her parents received life in solitary confinement, and the others all received life in prison. Between that and the small sparks of protest from within the vampire community and the fact that no slayer other than Jade felt comfortable enough to live within our city yet, I had reached my limit.

I wanted so badly for my dreams of our united future to come true, so I had to leave myself little reminders of the possibility of success. There was a sticky note on my bathroom mirror that I read each morning. *Each day is a step closer to achieving unity,* is what it read, and that sentiment kept me going on the really rough days.

Lo's squeal of excitement pulled me from my thoughts, and I grabbed a tissue, dabbing at the damp corners of my eyes to not fuck up the beautiful makeup job she'd done for me.

"That's my girl!" she yelled as she climbed off the bed, allowing Jade to sit up and take the shot.

Her face twisted up as she threw it back, and I couldn't help but laugh and grab one of the lime slices by me, throwing it in her lap as a small act of mercy.

Alexandra's stomach was probably so thankful to not be subjected to this again.

She shoved the lime into her mouth as a shiver ran through her body. She spit the fruit into her hands before saying, "Fuck, I don't know why you guys always insist on tequila shots. Like seriously, do you hate yourselves or something? There are much better options out there."

As the sound of music from our backyard kicked up a notch, playing the song that signaled the beginning of our ceremony, I quickly downed my last shot as Lo responded.

"You know damn well it's a tradition that started at my wedding, and it's now being upheld for Alina's! Don't for a second think we won't be doing it at yours and Alexandra's, Missy," she sassed, helping pull Jade to her feet before fussing with her hair to ensure it looked perfect.

I smiled at that notion. I couldn't have asked for a better core group of friends. Despite Alexandra not being able to make it today due to an important mission, I knew her soul was here with us to celebrate.

They both looked stunning, wearing blood-red, shimmering gowns that contrasted my wedding dress. My choice might shock some, but if they knew me at all, it really was the perfect dress for me.

A groan spilled from Jade's lips as she adjusted her top, pulling her breasts up to be on full display. "I'm so far from a wedding it isn't even funny, but maybe I'll be swept off my feet in a whirlwind romance like you, Lo. I still can't believe you got married before Alina."

Lo reapplied her lipstick, pressing her lips together before opening them with a pop as she winked at Jade in the mirror. "What can I say? Oleander is a man who knows what he wants—and that's me."

It was a fact that my mates had relentlessly reminded me of each time I pushed our own wedding back. My focus had felt so torn between the trial, my job with task enforcement, and helping out the academy when I could that our wedding had taken a back seat, until the day that Dev set me straight, reminding me that tomorrow wasn't guaranteed and that I needed to put my own wants and needs first.

It was two months ago that I finally brought in the wedding planner. We didn't leave the house for a week straight, getting absolutely everything chosen and the vendors set up all in one go. The only reason we even had to wait two months was for my wedding dress to be made.

I'd snuck into Ordinarius with Jade and Lo—with Dev delighting in adding input in my mind—to have the wedding dress shopping day of my dreams. It took forever, but I eventually found a dress that was the perfect shape and in the material I wanted—all that was missing was my one special request for the dress. It had cost a small fortune to have the changes made and the entire order expedited, but as I stood up and took in my final look in the full-length mirror, I knew it was worth it.

The black wedding gown was tight and figure-hugging, with a corset-style top and an intricate lace overlay that was detailed with delicate floral embroidery. The skirt flowed from my hips in an A-line style, with countless waves of the same lace detailing fluttering over a light and billowy tulle underskirt that gave it a look of fullness and grace.

Lo had braided my hair into a loose fishtail that I pulled to rest over the side of my neck, loving the way she'd left out a few loose, face-framing curls. It was simple and elegant, just like the smokey eyeshadow she'd applied at my request, along with the soft pink lip, which finished off the look.

I just hoped that my three future husbands agreed.

Both of my friends came to stand at my back, smiling so fucking big that my nerves disappeared, which no amount of tequila could have done.

You look absolutely breathtaking, Alina.

Thank you, Dev. Are you all set?

Dev has demanded to be placed in a seat like a guest, despite seeing through my own eyes and only having a vague sense of her surroundings without that ability. We'd given her the best spot in the front row, right next to where my bridesmaids were going to stand.

Wherever you chose to place me is perfect. Thank you for giving into my silly demands.

It's not silly, Dev. You're one of my closest friends and have been there through it all with us. I'm honored to have you here with us today.

I love you.

I love you too.

"Let's get you married, Al," Lo announced softly before guiding me out the door.

Everything in me wanted to reach out through

my bonds to check on how my men were doing as we headed down the staircase, but we'd agreed to keep our bonds closed until after I made my appearance at the start of the aisle. No words were allowed until our vows were exchanged, but we agreed that we could let our feelings through.

It was one of the very few traditions we were actually sticking to, having immediately vetoed the whole *not spending the night before the wedding together* one the second I'd pathetically attempted to kick them out of our bedroom last night. I honestly don't even know why I tried.

As the wedding coordinator gave Jade the go-ahead to walk down the aisle, my oldest friend blew me a kiss. "I'll see you out there."

Lo quickly pulled me in for a hug, whispering in my ear, "I know we're about to both be married gals, but I just want you to know that we will forever be Lo and Al—to the end. I love you."

"Shit, Lo," I choked out as she backed away and prepared to head down the aisle. "You're going to make me ruin my makeup before I even get out there."

With a wink at me, she quickly sassed me right out of my emotional state as she said, "Oh, let's not pretend that we don't know they all love the sight of your makeup smeared for them."

And with that, she was off, leaving me shaking my head and chuckling.

Your mates tell you that you're their dirty little whore *one* time in bed—with your lipstick smeared across your face and mascara tears streaming down your face—and you'll never live it down.

A smirk tilted the corner of my mouth up. Having that moment thrown at me would bother me if I didn't enjoy being whatever the hell they wanted me to be on any given night.

The coordinator handed me my bouquet of white roses with a pat on the shoulder. "You look beautiful, Alina. Head on out there and claim your mates."

I gave her the biggest smile, and she gathered my train behind me as I walked toward my future. As I rounded the corner, I gasped, coming into view of the most beautiful sight I'd ever laid eyes on. The choice to have the wedding at night, with countless string lights running through the massive oak tree that served as the backdrop of our ceremony, was the best decision I could have made.

The lights cast a stunning glow alongside the hundreds of candles and tea lights scattered around the three men standing at the end of the black satin path.

The music changed, announcing my arrival, and I opened my bond up to my mates the second our gazes met. It took approximately three seconds for my tears to start as I saw each of them wiping at their own eyes, their love and awe flowing through our connection.

I didn't bother wiping the tears away as I took the steps down the path that led to the loves of my life. To my mates, the ones fated for my soul as I was for theirs.

It felt like it took an eternity to get to them as I passed by the guests in a blur. When I was close enough to hand off my flowers to Lo, they each stepped down to help me up the steps to our altar.

Butterflies exploded in my stomach at finally being here in this moment with them.

"Please have a seat," the officiant's voice boomed as I took my designated spot, and they returned to their own.

I swear I didn't hear anything, zoning out at the beginning of the ceremony, completely lost in their gazes and the bubble of love around us, until the officiant cleared his throat softly at me and offered me a smile of understanding. "We're ready for your vows, Alina."

"Phew," I exhaled before attempting to recall the words I wanted to say to them, gaining a little chuckle from my mates as they grinned from ear to ear at me.

I felt tongue-tied just from staring at them in their black suits, gazing at me like I hung the stars in the sky.

Glancing out at the crowd for the first time, I announced, "With our union being unique and not wanting to make the ceremony an hour long, we've decided that my vows will be the only ones said out loud during the ceremony. No pressure, right?"

My little joke at the end warmed up the crowd, and I was met with a sea of smiles and laughter as I turned back to face my mates.

It was a decision we made together based on what felt right for us. Later tonight, they would read me their vows in private, but it was important for me to tell the world exactly how I felt about them during our ceremony.

I was the one who struggled with words of affirmation and openly stating my feelings, but I was working on it. Reading my vows—stating my feelings so completely and publicly—was a huge step for me, and it was one that I was more than thrilled to take. They deserved this and so much more for the way they'd supported my growth over the past three years.

"Andrei, Drake, and Lincoln," I started, addressing them in the order they stood before me and staring into each pair of eyes as I did. "I struggled so many nights, agonizing over the right words to use to put my love for you into both a cohesive sentence and something long enough to be considered vows."

Chuckles sounded once more, but I buckled in, ready to bare my soul. To the universe. To the world. And to my mates.

I licked my lips before continuing, hating the way my throat was already tightening with emotion before I even got the real words out.

"The truth is that our love can't be defined by words. It can't be contained and trapped in a little ball for me to describe. The love that we share is something our souls were destined for, just waiting for the perfect moment for us all to come into existence and together at the same time."

They each nodded at me in agreement, eyes misting with tears as I croaked, "Our love is one that will follow us beyond this life and into the next because it's a love so great it can't possibly be explored and felt to the deepest extent in just one lifetime."

A tear rolled down my cheek as I let out a shaky breath.

"Each day, you all show me that it's possible to fall deeper and deeper in love. At this point, I've given up on the notion that each day lived with love in my heart for you all is the maximum level that I can reach—because you all continue to shatter those glass ceilings with your love, patience, and desire to make sure I wake up and fall asleep each day with a smile on my face."

My lips pinched together as the waterworks really started, my throat growing thick with emotion. "So how does one sum all of that up into words?" I asked, shrugging gently and sniffling. "I can't. And I'm so damn happy that I can't because I don't want a love that fits into a mold. I want our unique love for the rest of eternity."

As I came to the end of my vows, they stepped forward, making me laugh through the tears as our officiant put a hand up, stopping them in their tracks. "Woah there, let me get to the 'I Do's' first, shall we? I promise it's happening right now."

I'm pretty sure Lincoln actually growled at him,

and if Drake's gentle elbow to his side was any indication, I was correct.

"Alina, do you take each of these men to be your husbands and fated mates, in this lifetime and the next?"

I grinned at each of them, sending my love through the bond individually before saying, "I do!"

"Lincoln, do you take Alina to be your wife and fated mate, in this lifetime and the next?"

A large grin took over his face as he nodded. "I do, Princess."

"Drake, do you take Alina to be your wife and fated mate, in this lifetime and the next?"

Fresh tears streamed down his face, catching in his beard as he nodded enthusiastically, his voice cracking slightly. "I do, *Comoroă*."

"Andrei, do you take Alina to be your wife and fated mate, in this lifetime and the next?"

My final mate drew a deep breath before smiling and running his eyes along my face like he was staring at the most exquisite artwork he'd ever seen. "I do. For forever and a day."

We didn't even wait for the officiant to announce it. No, I was kissing them all before he could even yell, "I now pronounce you husbands and wife!"

Before I lost myself in their touches, I sent one final thought to all of them.

For forever and a day.

THE END.

FLIP to the end for chapter one of Monsters Within, which is Alexandra's story.

Want to read about the other students Alina met or the Carmina Witch sector?

Alexandra's story - Order here!

Deva's (Witch at DIA) story- Order here!

Curious about Alora's parents who run Hell in this world? Read their series here:

Monarchs of Hell (Complete series)

Insurrection: mybook.to/Monarchs1

Imbalance: mybook.to/Monarchs2

Inheritance: mybook.to/Monarchs3

BOOKS BY R.L. CAULDER

<u>Blood Oath (Completed Series)</u>

Bite of Loyalty: <u>mybook.to/bite1</u>

Bite of Betrayal: <u>mybook.to/bite2</u>

Bite of Vengeance: <u>mybook.to/bite3</u>

Bite of Justice: <u>mybook.to/bite4</u>

<u>The Creatures We Crave</u>

Monsters Within: <u>mybook.to/MonstersWithin</u>

Monsters Below: <u>mybook.to/MonstersBelow</u>

Monsters Above: <u>mybook.to/MonstersAbove</u>

<u>The Vampyres' Source (Completed Series)</u>

Co-write with M. Sinclair

Ruthless Blood: <u>mybook.to/Ruthless1</u>

Ruthless War: <u>mybook.to/Ruthless2</u>

Ruthless Love: <u>mybook.to/Ruthless3</u>

<u>The Pack Prophecy (Completed Series)</u>

Outcast: <u>mybook.to/Outcast</u>

Outlaw: mybook.to/OutlawPP

Oracle: mybook.to/OraclePP

Darkness Rising (Completed Series)

Desolation: mybook.to/Desolation

Detonation: mybook.to/Detonation

Devastation: mybook.to/DevastationDR

Monster's Naughty List (Standalone book)

mybook.to/Naughtylist

Inferno (Standalone book)

Co-write with M. Sinclair

mybook.to/InfernoMC

Captured by the Monsters (Standalone book)

Co-write with M.J. Marstens

mybook.to/CapturedMonsters

ABOUT R.L. CAULDER

R.L. Caulder is a USA Today bestselling author who lives in her writing cave away from the intense heat of the Florida sun with her husband and furry writing assistants, MeowMeow and Winrey. Life is never boring for R.L., who has hundreds of imaginary friends constantly vying for her attention and begging for their stories to be told.

If you're looking for ways to interact with R.L., you can find her on Facebook in her group:

The Cauldron: R.L. Caulder Reader Group

ALEXANDRA

THE CREATURES WE CRAVE: BOOK ONE

I knew life wasn't sunshine and rainbows for everyone, but eventually the clouds always broke, revealing the sunlight once more for them. But in my case, the darkness that seemed to follow me never cleared.

I had learned a long time ago, life wasn't fair, and at some point, I just accepted it.

The only bright spot was when I was able to climb into my bed, crack open a spiral notebook, and forget reality even existed while being transported into the world I created when I put my pen to paper.

I poured all of my despair and desire onto those sheets. The ink was my pain, and the pages were my savior.

It's where I found myself now, contemplating

the events of the day and how I would cope with them. I was lounging on my bed in an oversized Aerosmith t-shirt I'd found at the thrift shop and some black sleep shorts.

Shoving the rest of my chocolate chip cookie into my mouth, I grabbed the plastic cup filled with the delicious delicacy known as RumChata. Taking a gulp of the cinnamon alcohol, I swallowed down the lump of cookie that lodged itself in my throat before setting the cup back down on my nightstand.

The alcohol had been given to me as a bribe to not tell on the girl across the hall for smoking a joint. I honestly didn't care what she did—I wouldn't have turned her in anyway, but I wouldn't turn my nose up at alcohol.

Despite not having any friends here, I kept to myself... it was just easier. My life had enough chaos without me creating enemies. I had my own shit to worry about. If the girl wanted to smoke pot to get through her days, who was I to judge? We all had our own ways of coping.

The RumChata left a trail of light heat in its wake as I reached for my black spiral notebook that had seen better days. The edges of the pages curled slightly from being bent a bit when I wrote at odd angles. Flipping to the next blank page near the back of the book, I realized that I would need to grab another one soon and add this full one to the plastic bin beneath my bed. That bin held the only things in the world I cared about, the only things that held any value for me.

As a ward of the state, I hadn't enjoyed many luxuries in life growing up. Even now, being on an academic scholarship for my junior year at a small private college, I wasn't afforded much. *The single dorm room was definitely a plus, though.*

I couldn't dwell on the fact that all the possessions I cared about could fit into one measly bin beneath my bed. One day, things would be different—that day just wasn't today. I was what you could call a "pessimistic optimist."

My scholarship covered my classes, school materials, boarding, and a small stipend for food. I'd be the first to admit I had a pretty shit diet. I wouldn't eat all day, then I'd use my budgeted allowance for the day to order a large pizza and cookies and binge eat as I wrote through the night.

Another terrible habit was my almost non-existent sleep schedule, and I often found myself cursing the first rays of morning light as they streamed in through my small window. They took me away from my fantasy world filled with delicious men I was unhealthily obsessed with, signaling that I'd once again be heading to classes running on fumes.

Often I dreamt of being one of the supernatural creatures of the world instead of an isolated, forgotten human stuck in an endless loop that kept reminding me of my place in life.

But unfortunately, this seemed to be the hand I'd been dealt. I just needed to find a way to make the most of it.

That didn't stop me, though, from checking my teeth to see if they'd elongated to sharp points like a vampire's, trying to conjure fire into existence in my hand like a witch, or wishing I'd grown a pair of demon horns overnight.

Maybe I was just a late bloomer in the supernatural community? At least, that's what I liked to tell myself when I found myself sinking in the bleakness of my life.

Grabbing a pen with a slightly gnawed black cap from my nightstand, I backed into the corner of my bed against the wall, a cozy space where I had my pillows arranged and smashed in a nest of sorts to engulf me. Drawing my knees up, I rested my notebook against them, closed my eyes, and tipped my head back to rest against the wall, thinking of where I would be transported to this time.

It was time to cut myself loose from reality and escape to the world between my pages. A world that inspired awe and forged hope within my soul. Hope that one day the world I lived in would be a better place.

My fantasy world was one in which I righted the wrongs of the world. Where the monsters most people were afraid of helped me hunt down the true bad guys—the humans.

Because I can assure you, my monsters were angels in comparison to the true evil that lurked in my reality. Humans just happened to wear skin suits that were more pleasing to the eye.

Closing my eyes, I allowed my mind to drift to the image of my monsters, sinking into the alternate life I'd created for myself.

At first, when I'd created them, there had been nothing beautiful about my monsters, but they had morphed in my mind over the years. Before I learned how to write, I drew them as faceless shadow creatures draped in the fabric of black cloaks with ripped edges at the bottom. They moved in the darkness, shifting with the shadows, undeniably hidden from the human eye.

Then, as I wrote them in stories instead of drawings, when they weren't traveling in the darkness, the lower halves of their bodies were still mostly swirling shadows, but there was a section in the middle of their chests that thrummed with a steady glow, like a human had their heart.

Each of my three monsters had a different color that emanated from the piece of them I liked to think of as their soul, spreading into their necks and up into their faces like veins beneath the surface.

Lucien was red.

Elwin was green.

Kylo was blue.

Then, to top it all off, they had four arms, two on each side, with razor sharp claws at the tips of their fingers. Some might find them disconcerting, being so devoid of humanoid features, but it's what I loved about them. What you saw was what you got, unlike humans.

I had met too many dark, ugly, twisted humans for me to trust them.

They'd smile to your face to placate you, whispering the words you wanted to hear, all while taking what they wanted before leaving behind a husk of a person.

The ones who stole.

The ones who raped.

The ones who thought they deserved everything simply because they breathed.

In my fantasy world, my monsters and I snuffed the arrogance and entitlement out of every single one of those fuckers. Sometimes discretion was needed, so, in addition to their monster forms, they had a human form so they could blend in with society and be at my side.

Which brought me to the task at hand. Opening my eyes, I thought of where I wanted to begin with this one. Today's chapter was about the Dean of Students who had lifted my skirt this afternoon and told me he'd forget the claims of me cheating on my essay if I *helped* him.

I hadn't cheated.

There was no need to when academics were a natural gift of my mind. The only way I was even able to attend this college was due to the academic scholarship I'd been awarded. Without it, I'd be on the streets without a penny to my name, like most kids after they aged out of the system.

There was definitely no way I'd risk any of that by cheating on a dumb creative writing essay that I could ace without struggling.

The problem was that Chloe Blufount didn't like that I continuously ranked above her for the top spot in the undergraduate class for English majors. Our creative writing professor instituted a public ranking board to encourage excellence, and with my talent for writing, I edged Chloe out every year. But Chloe was a girl who was used to getting her way, especially since her father's money usually got her everything else she wanted. He could buy her lip injections, lash extensions, a constant fake spray tan, and her continuously revolving hair colors, but he'd never be able to buy her top rank in our class.

I was proud of that.

So this was how she got me out of the way instead. Feeding the skeevy dean lies, knowing full well what his reputation was. Chloe was one of the monsters beneath a pretty human skin suit, offering me on a silver platter to a man who took what wasn't freely given, knowing I had no one to help me fight my battles other than myself.

In reality, I had smacked his hand away lightly, told him I'd take the zero on the assignment, and quietly left his office, not wanting to ignite the temper I'd heard about many times.

It finally came to me, how I wanted this scene to go. The specific way I wanted the dean to suffer. I let the ink glide on the page, closing my eyes and summoning my bloodthirsty monster to reenact the scene in the manner I truly wanted.

Lucien.

He'd slaughter for those he loved without blinking. Touch what was his and die a painful death as a result. It was that simple to him.

The scene was finally set. There I was, sitting with my legs crossed in the chair in front of the dean's oak desk, with the dean standing and leaning against the corner of it, eyeing me like a pig.

As Lucien stepped from the shadows in the corner of the office, his fingertips gleamed like freshly sharpened obsidian daggers. His form shifted as he approached slowly and intentionally, like a predator stalking his prey, confidence and danger radiating off of him in waves. His blood-red eyes with black slits were pinned on his target with unwavering intensity.

Truly, he embodied the creature of nightmares kids would fear coming from the shadowed corners of their rooms.

Just as the perv put his hand on my exposed leg and drew it up toward my skirt, as he had in reality, Lucien tutted at him. "That simply won't do. The only person allowed to touch my angel is me."

The dean stood, frozen in fear of my monster,

and I smiled wickedly when his beige dress pants darkened and the scent of urine permeated the air. All it took was Lucien's talons touching his skin in the faintest whisper of a touch.

The dean knew he had just become the prey.

The shadows on Lucien's face parted to reveal his lips as he smiled at the dean, putting his rows of sharp teeth on display. The dean screamed, begging for mercy, in the seconds before his hands were swiftly cleaved from his wrists.

Maybe that act should have scared me—it was what I truly wanted, and craving that type of violence wasn't normal. But instead, it unfurled a sense of justice and satisfaction within me, perhaps even a hint of desire towards Lucien for the vicious move.

Alright, it was more than a hint of desire.

It wouldn't be the first time their possessive and sometimes barbaric actions had turned me on. But it wasn't a surprise because I had written them to be exactly like that.

The thing was—my creations weren't just monsters. They were my soul mates, and I had created them to be extremely protective and territorial over me. Something I'd lacked in my life growing up. They all had distinctively different personalities, but their underlying love and need to keep me safe shone brightly through their shadowy depths.

The dean's screams echoed through the expanse of his office, but no one came to his rescue. No one could save him—he was damned from the start of my story.

He fell to his knees as blood poured in rivulets from his severed wrists, pooling beneath him in an ever-expanding crimson lake. Snot poured from his nose as he sobbed and begged, "Please, spare me. I'm sorry. I'm so sorry."

Narrowing my eyes as I stood from my chair, I planted the bottom of my boot on his chest before kicking him backwards. "Too bad you won't be able to say sorry to all of your other victims," I sneered. Then, huffing out a dry laugh, I added, "Though, your death will be enough of an apology."

As the words left my lips, Lucien towered over the dean before ramming the tips of his pointer fingers into his eye sockets. The dean only screamed for a few seconds before the bliss of silence descended through the small office with his death.

I soaked the moment in, smiling smugly at his fate. He wouldn't be able to abuse his position of power again.

Meanwhile, Lucien retracted his talons from the

dean and grabbed a handkerchief from the desk, wiping off his top hands' talons with his lower two before tossing the rag onto the dean's body. Dramatically, he rolled his eyes and murmured, "I hate when they make me get my hands so dirty."

A true laugh burst from me as I called him on his bullshit. "You're such a liar. You get upset when you *don't* get to handle our situations this way," I reminded him as I leaned back onto the desk with my hands on the edge. "Though I'm sure Kylo and Elwin would love to hear if you're changing your ways," I added teasingly. "You'd make their lives so much easier."

It was his turn to laugh, and the sound truly made my heart skip a beat. I lived for their love and joy—it fed my own.

"Don't let Kylo lie to you either, angel," he rebutted. "He'd be bored if he wasn't constantly trying to contain my urges under the bloodhaze."

As Lucien came to float in front of me, leaning in close, I widened my eyes and fake pouted. "But what about poor Elwin who has to deal with calming Kylo down when you inevitably go against his commands?"

He paused as if truly giving it a thought before chuckling. "Yeah, I feel bad for the bastard, but we all know I'm not going to stop. No one fucks with you or my brothers and gets away with only a slap on the wrist."

The reminder of his wrath had my eyes falling down to the dean, and my body shivered at the memory of his touch on my leg.

Lucien sensed my distress, his voice dropping low as he whispered, "You're okay now, angel. He'll never touch you again. You are ours."

The possessiveness of his words, combined with the deep tones of his voice, made heat pool between my legs. An ache began to build, demanding I find a way to satisfy it.

I had yet to bring myself to cross the line of being intimate with my creatures as I wrote my stories, but today felt like the day that was going to change. I needed a little something extra to cheer me up after having to swallow my outrage at the dean's actions. I'd wanted to punch him in the mouth and tell him where he could shove it with his suggestions, but seeing as I couldn't give in to that desire... I'd give in to this one instead.

The Creatures We Crave

Monsters Within: mybook.to/MonstersWithin